"In this gripping, poignant novel by Ginger Park, a Korean family is torn apart by Japanese and Russian rule during World War II and sacrificial love, yet held together by faith, food, and memories. Miyook's family owns a bustling department store in the city of Sinuiju in northern Korea, but communism forces her family to leave everything behind to escape over mountains and a river to freedom in the south. On her journey, Miyook learns that small gestures are never forgotten. I love this story."

— Tina Cho, author of *The Ocean Calls* and *Rice from Heaven*

"How do you tell a tale of war, the separation of family and country, of heroes and villains, and make it sound like poetry? Ginger Park has woven a beautiful and heartbreaking story of Korea in the twentieth century in *The Hundred Choices Department Store*. Her details of food and family traditions are as heartwarming as a bowl of steamy homemade noodles. The novel is an excellent introduction to life in Korea during World War II and the civil war that followed. A beautiful book."

— Kitty Felde, author of *Welcome to Washington Fina Mendoza* and *State of the Union: a Fina Mendoza Mystery*

"History and heart intertwine in this gripping, deeply felt novel about a divided family in a divided country. As World War II comes to a close in northern Korea, Miyooki must confront external danger--occupying Russian soldiers, vicious border patrols—and internal doubt and grief to find her true place in a changing land. This book sings of the beauties of an old way of life—and of hope and possibility."

— Mary Quattlebaum, author of *Pirate vs. Pirate*

"This beautifully written, heart-wrenching coming-of-age story speaks to the enduring power of familial bonds and the resiliency of the human spirit. As her world is destroyed by tyranny, subjugation, and agonizing separation, Miyook learns that a small act of kindness can have enormous consequences. The heightened pathos of deftly crafted scenes will inspire empathy and compassion for the plight of refugees. A riveting, timely, humanizing account of risking everything for freedom."

— Jama Rattigan, author of *Dumpling Soup*

"Ginger Park weaves her family's story into a compelling novel reaching far beyond battle dates and casualties—a reminder that losses from conflict have a lasting impact, even on resilient children, and political boundaries often draw red lines through the heart."

— Karen Leggett Abouraya, author of *Hands Around the Library: Protecting Egypt's Treasured Books* and *Malala Yousafzai: Warrior with Words*

"A fantastic middle-grade historical novel that takes place during World War II and the tumultuous years leading up to the Korean War, set on the Korean Peninsula. Drawn from stories of the author's family, *The Hundred Choices Department Store* is a richly detailed book that chronicles a harrowing era in Korean history. This book does a great job of illustrating the hard choices so many families had to make—stay in a familiar place that has been turned upside down and face danger at the hands of people who had once been allies or venture into the unknown. This is a wonderfully written, heart-wrenching tale of family and resilience!"

— Meg Wessell, blogger, *A Bookish Affair*

THE HUNDRED CHOICES DEPARTMENT STORE

Ginger Park

Fitzroy Books

Copyright © 2022 Ginger Park. All rights reserved.

Published by Fitzroy Books
An imprint of
Regal House Publishing, LLC
Raleigh, NC 27587
All rights reserved

https://fitzroybooks.com

Printed in the United States of America

ISBN -13 (paperback): 9781646032129
ISBN -13 (epub): 9781646032136
Library of Congress Control Number: 2021935999

All efforts were made to determine the copyright holders and obtain their permissions in any circumstance where copyrighted material was used. The publisher apologizes if any errors were made during this process, or if any omissions occurred. If noted, please contact the publisher and all efforts will be made to incorporate permissions in future editions.

Interior and cover design by Lafayette & Greene
Cover image © by C. B. Royal

Regal House Publishing, LLC
https://regalhousepublishing.com

The following is a work of fiction created by the author. All names, individuals, characters, places, items, brands, events, etc. were either the product of the author or were used fictitiously. Any name, place, event, person, brand, or item, current or past, is entirely coincidental.

All rights reserved. No part of this publication may be reproduced, stored in a retrieval system, or transmitted, in any form or by any means, electronic, mechanical, photocopying, recording, or otherwise, without the prior permission of Regal House Publishing.

Printed in the United States of America

To my beautiful mother who blessed me
with more stories than I could ever write

"It is during our darkest moments
that we must focus to see the light."

— Aristotle

PROLOGUE

December arrives with cold winds and the promise of knee-deep snows. I sit up in bed and gaze into the mirror, wondering if this will be my last winter. My old bones tell me it just might be. I've been counting the days for quite some time now. I am, after all, eighty-nine years old. Ninety in Korean years (as we celebrate the first birthday on the day one is born). Oma would never recognize the old woman looking back at me. In her eyes, I'm forever a teenage girl.

I hear my daughter calling after her restless nineteen-year-old son who is out the door.

"Carson, come back here now!"

My grandson reminds me of Hoon, my tortured baby-faced brother, who lived in the shadow of Hwan, his fraternal twin. But I suspect Carson will find his way in the world. If only Hoon had been given the chance... With bittersweet thoughts, my eyes turn to the gold bamboo-framed needlepoint canvas on the wall. The embroidered scene comes alive in vibrant color—beneath a canopy of fiery persimmon trees, a little boy eats sweet fruit under a night sky aglow with a full *Chuseok* moon, the symbol of happiness. My heart skips a beat. For although my family before this one is long gone, memories are so close, I can almost touch them. Almost.

1

THE WAR EFFORT - 1944

Yes, Japan occupied my country, but not my heart…

Manchurian winds blew into Sinuiju, whistling December's arrival. The Amrok River was already an ice-skating rink, a winter paradise where children and lovebirds gathered like penguins on ice, carving out figure eights.

Ajumah, our housekeeper, lit up the *ondol*, the heating system, which kept the house warm throughout the winter months by way of a giant hearth that sent heat into underground piping, warming the floors. I placed my hands over the blazing fire, not wanting to go to school. Who could blame me? The Ichiban School was no longer a place of learning and no longer offered fun activities such as music, origami, and needlepoint art. In fact, my Chuseok moon project was far from finished when the war broke out. Our classroom teacher, whom we called *sensei*, told us to create a haiku on canvas, something meaningful to the heart. And, right then, nothing meant more to me than the Korean harvest holiday and paying my respects to ancestors under a full Chuseok moon. My sensei was blind to the meaning of my moon, thank God. Had he known, he would have raised his pointer stick like a weapon and punished me with a good whipping. Expressing my Korean-ness in his Japanese-controlled school was a forbidden act, a treasonous act. But as Hoon always told me, I *was* Korean, *not* Japanese, no matter how hard my sensei tried to brainwash me into believing otherwise. We learned the Japanese language and Japanese history, and we bowed to a wall-sized portrait of

Emperor Hirohito. We were assigned Japanese names. Mine was Himeko, a meaningless label for a girl christened Miyook, which means *beautiful pearl*. Oma always said, "At home you are Korean, you are our little Miyooki Pang, our good Christian daughter. But once you venture out the door, you must bite your lip and accept who you are in the outside world: Himeko who honors Shinto."

Two worlds. Two identities.

Yes, Japan occupied my country, but not my heart.

The Japanese arrived on Korean shores in 1910, orchestrating a perfect takeover of our land and people. I tried to envision what life had been like before Japan's rule, when my maternal grandfather was the wealthiest landowner this side of the Kangnam mountain range. When villagers were potters and herbalists, and engaged in processions that danced through the countryside, chasing away evil spirits. When Chuseok was celebrated at the ancient Confucian temple under glowing lanterns, while musicians strummed their kayagums, the sweet notes floating through the cool autumn air.

It was hard to picture such a peaceful life.

Now, my Chuseok moon was lost in my closet among other unfinished projects like my silk painting and origami boat. I vowed to someday complete my haiku on canvas and proudly hang my embroidered moon on my bedroom wall as a reminder that I had survived the war effort.

School days were spent darning socks and stitching buttons onto military uniforms—for the war effort. We polished boots until our fingernails were black—for the war effort. In the spring, when we were supposed to send our origami boats down the new rushing river, we were squatting in the rice fields—for the war effort. Since food was rationed at school, lunch consisted of a single rice ball sprinkled with sesame seeds. At home, we prayed before meals, but when my sensei doled out his tray of rice balls at school, prayers were replaced with his daily rhetoric: *Eat sparingly, for our fighting soldiers need all our food to keep their bodies strong against the American devil!*

And all I could think about was my own hunger. Was I selfish? No. I was a thirteen-year-old Korean girl, and as Hoon always reminded me, no Japanese soldier was fighting on *my* behalf. Besides, if the Japanese were truly fighting, then why were kamikaze pilots hiding out at our school, their tiny planes shrouded by underbrush, while the rumbling American B-29 fighter planes flew overhead leaving trails of smoke in the sky?

"Because the Japs are losing the war, little one!" Hoon insisted with glee. "They were fools to bomb Pearl Harbor and think the Americans would sit still and do nothing."

At first, the American presence terrified me, especially after my sensei drilled it into my head that bombs would soon drop from American planes and wipe us off the map. Whenever B-29ers were overhead, sirens would go off, signaling us to retreat to our shelters. We would take cover, huddling in fetal positions. But the bombs never dropped, and eventually, we stopped hiding. Over time, the sirens and the rumbling of the B-29s, with their trails of smoke across the sky, grew peripheral to our lives.

If not for the morning meals Oma always cooked me—seaweed soup, fish pancakes, egg pie, aromatic sprouts—and the lemon candies she tucked inside my pocket for the long walks home in the dark, I wouldn't have survived the war effort. Still, my parents would never grant my wish to skip school. They knew the consequences.

First, my sensei would show up at our doorstep with a suspicious eye. A burning interrogation would follow: *Why was Himeko not in school today? Is she sick, dying, or just hiding from her duties to the Motherland? Tell her to think about our great warriors who are perishing on land and sea and in the air fighting to protect her from the American devil. I expect Himeko at school tomorrow.*

Secondly, at school the next day, Principal Shimmura

would ridicule me in front of my classmates, and my sensei would punish the whole class by serving half-sized rice balls and skipping over me altogether with a hateful glare. Even my friends, upset at the hostile environment, would banish me from their lives.

Alas, there was no escaping the day ahead.

"Have a good day, Miyooki!" Oma called out to me.

But I was already out the door, fighting the bitterly cold wind.

Sometimes Oma's cheerful sendoff put me in a bad mood. She knew a day of meaningless drudgery awaited me. Sometimes I thought she loved her cherished orphans more than her own children. Where was she when I ate a rotten rice ball and retched my guts out the whole way home from school? With the orphans. Where was she when I pricked my finger over and over with a dirty sewing needle that caused painful swelling and infection? With the orphans. Maybe I *was* selfish. Sometimes I needed Oma to love and comfort *me*, but her heart, it seemed, belonged to the orphans.

"Have pity on Oma's heart," Hoon said. "Remember, little one, she lost three children before you were born. She couldn't save her own, but she has saved many orphans."

I had heard the stories of two stillborn infants and a two-year-old daughter who died of whooping cough. Oma never spoke of her dead babies, but I often wondered if her lack of appetite and daily battles with migraines were caused by these ghost children.

The Ichiban School was a three-mile trek across an icy path along a busy road. On a spring day, it was an easy hour-and-a-half walk from home. But come winter, I left before sunrise, taking small, careful steps in the dark. Clad in three layers of outerwear and a double wool scarf across my face, the well-below freezing temperatures cut through me like icicles. Even with friends and classmates, the walks to school were long and quiet with the stars over our heads and the bustling shopping district yet to open for business. But walks home were joyful because I could mark off another day at the Ichiban School and all my favorite shops were open—the Duk Jip, which offered the sweetest red bean paste *mochi* and savory pork buns made fresh daily by Mr. Lim, the cook and baker. Next to the Duk Jip was the Udon House, the Korean community haunt where Hoon and I met once a week—every Wednesday at six o'clock sharp—for spirited conversation about life and dreams over bowls of freshly made noodles that were always long and chewy and swimming in a warm fragrant broth. A tantalizing mountain of sliced scallions and marinated beef completed the meal. At our table with a view of the stars, food and secrets were always shared.

"Miyooki, someday I'm going to marry Kyung Kim," Hoon once vowed.

Kyung Kim was one of Hwan's castoffs—a Korean girl he dated back in high school, a sweet girl he promised the world before breaking her heart when he met the lovely Yumi Mitsuwa from Tokyo.

"You don't even know Kyung," I protested. "And besides, of all the Korean girls in town, why would you want to marry someone who dated your own brother?"

"I knew Kyung in high school," Hoon maintained. "She is bright, beautiful..."

"And loved Hwan," I said.

Hoon chuckled. "Okay, Little Miss Expert on Love, who is my baby sister going to marry someday?"

"Well...I don't know about marriage, but I do like Jin-Su at church."

"Jin-Su?" Hoon mulled, rubbing his chin thoughtfully. "Oh, the skinny choir boy with the red cheeks?" he asked with a laugh.

I nodded. "Yes, that one. He has a very beautiful voice."

"Miyooki, you are far too tall for that pipsqueak!"

"And you daydream about girls you will never know!"

Next to the Udon House was the prize of the shopping district: The Hundred Choices Department Store, whose neon sign lit up the town at night. The glitzy store with gleaming hardwood floors catered to wealthy Japanese men and women who easily dropped one hundred yen without batting an eye. Luxury choices included expensive jewelry encrusted with sapphires, emeralds, rubies, and diamonds, and glittering with every color of the rainbow. Eighteen-karat gold watches lined the glass cases and the heavy scent of expensive perfume and cologne from Tokyo to Paris thickened the air. The Hundred Choices Department Store also sold suits for every occasion, leather shoes and boots, cashmere sweaters, winter undergarments, wool socks, hats, and scarves. My parents and Hwan owned the department store, along with a minority investor by the name of Dai Takagi. Hwan had met Dai at college in Japan. Both men were world travelers and talked of their desire for wealth over endless carafes of warm sake. The Hundred Choices Department Store was a mere steppingstone to the international investments they had planned together. For Hoon, the general manager, the department store gave him a life, a reason to wake up every morning and look forward to another day.

I only met Dai a few times, as he was a mysterious figure who rarely visited our home, but he was memorable all the same. A striking man of distinguished airs, his muscular build made him seem taller than his actual height of five foot six. He wore tailored suits cut from the finest silk, and his slicked-back hair mimicked the American matinee idols Hwan always talked about. Dai sauntered through the department store as if he were the emperor himself, expecting the employees to bow at his feet, reprimanding Hoon for this and that. *The window displays are shabby! There is so much dust! And why is that decrepit old woman working the cosmetic counter? Put her in the shoe department where she belongs!*

Needless to say, whenever Dai's name came up around

Hoon, his eyes bulged out and his round baby face turned red with rage. "All he does is insult the employees and badger me for monthly gross sales receipts! Have you seen him take cash out of the register? He is a money monger who takes advantage of his Korean employees' hard work!" he once spat. "Without his Jap blood running through his veins, he is nothing in this world! Nothing!"

Dai's partnership in the business drove a wedge between Hwan and Hoon. True, they were blood brothers, fraternal twins, but you would never know it. Both were handsome young men with Hwan the cultured and worldly one, while Hoon was a patriot who resented the Japanese presence in our country. He wasn't interested in seeing the world or doing business with what he called a *dirty Jap*. But as Apa explained to me, it had been a necessary decision to open the department store with a Japanese minority shareholder. "Less chance of meddlesome Japanese officials closing us down or demanding a portion of the profits," he said.

The truth was, my parents never uttered a disparaging word about Dai, but in their silence, I heard quiet resentment towards the irreverent Japanese man.

Hoon took great pride in his work. He didn't like leaving Sinuiju, but as the manager and sole purchaser of goods, he was forced to travel throughout Asia from Hong Kong to Singapore, and Europe too, in search of the trendiest clothes and accessories for his Japanese clientele. Upon his return, he was always proud of his newest finds—the delicate jade bracelets and satin purses, the faux-pearl cashmere sweaters, wool coats, and suits with international flair. Hoon never spoke of his travels, the places he visited, or the people he met.

Two brothers. Two worlds.

2

THE DYE FACTORY

I looked to the sky and quietly cursed the Japanese...

After our daily salute to Emperor Hirohito and the Motherland, our sensei stood before the class and made an announcement that summoned a gasp from me and my classmates. "For the next two weeks," he said, "you will be assigned to the dye factory. There is a shortage of workers as well as uniforms for our honored war fighters."

The dye factory! I had never entered the gray low-rise building on the other side of town, but I had seen its black smoke marring the sky and heard all the rumors about the grim fate of workers who fell into the boiling dye vats. If my sensei worried for us at all, he hid it well behind a steely expression. His unwavering loyalty to the Motherland was downright scary.

Hoon called the dye factory "Hell's Chamber," convinced as he was that rumors of Korean deaths were real. "Now all Jap uniforms are stained with Korean blood," he said, eyes flashing with fire, "not to mention flesh and bones!"

Hwan scoffed at his brother. "Baby sister," he told me, "don't listen to Hoon's stories. He was born with a chip on his shoulder. Listen to *me*. Anger will only eat at your heart like crows."

Yes, Hoon was a master storyteller, but I wouldn't agree or disagree with either of my brothers. At the age of twenty-five, they were both stubborn and saw the world very differently. While Hwan won the respect of the Japanese and had women swooning over him, Hoon was a loner. He always reminded me that, though the Japanese might look down on him, at six foot one, he was taller than every Japanese man he passed on the street and an inch taller than his own twin brother. While Hwan held a degree from a respected Japanese university, Hoon had barely completed his high school studies.

I once overheard Apa say, "Hwan is educated, a person of vision. Hoon is brilliant but lost."

Hoon not only spun tales of the Japanese, but of his own educational status.

"Hoon?" I asked him one day over a hot steaming bowl of noodle soup. "Why do you always tell your customers you went to college and won all kinds of academic awards when it isn't true?"

"Hush, little one," he said, lowering his voice to a whisper. "This is my secret. You must understand that my clients treat me with respect, honor, and power because they view me as an educated Korean man. If they knew the truth, they would spit on me, treat me like a leper or worse a Korean peasant."

Respect. Honor. Power.

A veil of lies.

I stirred my soup, the noodles snaking around my chopsticks as steam rose in my face like fog.

❧

After a two-mile trek across town, we arrived at the dye factory, which was far more dismal up close. My body ached, and I was tired and hungry, already craving one of Oma's delicious morning meals. I could almost taste her egg pie that was always hot from the steamer and flecked with chopped scallions and red pepper flakes. But when we entered the foul-smelling factory, my pain and hunger subsided at the sight of ghost-like children hunched over the iron vats, their small bodies bobbing up and down as they dunked sheets of white material into pools of dark blue dye—a surreal image that would haunt my sleep for many years to come. If Hoon was telling the truth, then it was the blood of Korean children that stained Japanese military uniforms, for there wasn't an adult factory worker in sight.

The young supervisor by the name of Mr. Lee handed out facemasks and rubber gloves before assigning us to our vats. He was a Korean man with superior airs and a face carved from chiseled stone. Yes, a cold, angular, merciless face. Hoon had warned me of his kind.

"They are worse than Japs, little one! They are traitors who sold their souls to the Devil!"

This was a perfect description for the insolent Mr. Lee. He surely ate three square meals a day, while the children under his supervision starved and toiled over the dye vats from sunrise to sunset.

To keep us focused on our work, my classmates and I were separated from one another.

"No talking allowed," Mr. Lee said in a low, threatening tone. He paced up and down the factory floor with a watchful eye, swinging a baton like a pendulum of death. No one spoke or made eye contact. The fear was palpable. It wouldn't surprise me if these small children were hiding bruises under their rags.

The boy at the vat beside me was pale and small, with blue-stained arms. I guessed him to be no more than twelve years old, but his gaunt face told a troubling story. For a time, we worked in silence, dunking sheets of material into the vats and hanging them on the liners overhead to dry. It wasn't long before my own arms were blue stained too. I was cold and lonely, and the fishy stench of dye sickened me.

Finally, Mr. Lee disappeared behind an office door, likely for a lunchbreak or a nap. When I was sure the coast was clear, I turned to the boy and whispered, "Hello." But he didn't hear me above the heavy clanking of factory machinery. So, I tapped his shoulder. "Hello," I said again.

The boy looked up at me with sweet, sad eyes, but turned

away without replying. He wasn't interested in knowing me or perhaps he knew Mr. Lee's rage firsthand. But I was determined to make a friend that day, to make my work at the dye factory bearable. When I offered the boy a lemon candy, his eyes lit up.

"I'm Miyook," I whispered.

The boy plucked the candy from my palm, gazing at it as if it were a sparkling crown jewel. Popping the candy into his mouth, he closed his eyes, feasting on its sweet tartness, sucking feverishly in complete rapture. Had Mr. Lee emerged from his office with his baton raised, I doubt the boy would have even noticed.

When the candy was gone, he opened his eyes and said, "Song-ho."

"Song-ho," I said. "That's a nice name." When he didn't respond, I asked, "So, Song-ho, where do you go to school?"

He squinted at me with a sideways look as if no one had ever asked him that question before. "No school here."

Did that mean Song-ho didn't go to school at all? I didn't ask. "How old are you?" I said, instead.

"Fifteen."

Fifteen? No, he couldn't be more than twelve! How was it possible that this little boy was older than me? Then I remembered Oma's orphans, all of them small, sad, and quiet. Last summer, an orphaned girl came to our house for the day. I didn't know her story, but I guessed her to be around nine years old. As with Song-ho, she didn't talk much, but she clung to me like the older sister she had always hoped for. We went outside to play, but she was drawn to Oma's lush flower garden. I plucked a pink lily and placed it in her hair. When she smiled, I saw an older girl, one with dreamless eyes.

I would later learn we were the same age.

Now, as I observed Song-ho, I did, indeed, see fifteen years in his ghost-like hollow face. "Where do you live?" I asked him.

Song-ho glanced down at the floor, as if ashamed. "Here," he whispered.

"*Here* as in the factory?"

"Yes."

I looked around. "Where in the factory?"

"In the dorm on the other side of the building."

"Where are your oma and apa?"

Song-ho's sudden frown broke my heart for I had seen the same expression many times before on the wistful faces of Oma's orphans who visited the church for our Open House holiday meals. The orphans always kept to themselves, sitting at one table, devouring their plates of food in silence. Clearly, Song-ho was an orphan too. He didn't want to talk about his parents, and I felt terrible for my nosiness.

Instead of answering my stupid question, he said, "May I have another candy?"

I smiled, emptying my pockets of lemon candies, which I placed in Song-ho's hands.

Eight hours later, I left the factory for the five-mile walk home with Song-ho on my mind. I wanted to know more about this fifteen-year-old boy who loved lemon candies. Why was he living at the factory? Where were his parents? What was his future? Many of these questions, I knew, would likely go unanswered.

Halfway home, my mind turned to my own tired body. I looked to the sky and quietly cursed the Japanese for the blisters on my feet, my blue-stained arms, and my aching back. I cursed Mr. Lee too. He was a traitor to his own people. Apa always called me his little *cheonsa*, but I didn't feel like an angel anymore. All my thoughts were gathered around hatred. Hatred for my sensei, my school, and every Japanese person who walked the earth; hatred for the cowardly Mr. Lee and all Koreans who betrayed their own. At that moment, only Song-ho and the other children of the dye factory found a place in my heart. My stomach hurt from hunger and felt sick with sadness. I had given Song-ho all my lemon candies and my rice ball too. It was the least I could do for the poor orphaned boy who lived in Hell's Chamber and worked the dye vats from dawn to dusk only to fall asleep to the sound of his own growling tummy.

Now I walked, heavy with guilt, knowing a hearty meal at the Udon House was just a few miles away.

Lights glowed from the Udon House with dreamlike effect, beckoning me inside. I was cold and numb with fatigue, but the sight of Hoon waiting for me at our table—the one by the window overlooking the street, under the stars—made me sigh with happiness. He sat cross-legged, sipping ginseng tea, tapping his perfect piano fingers nervously on the table. A gifted musician, Hoon was self-taught, shunning his piano teacher, who he claimed was an idiot. Yes, Hoon could play a song once and know it by heart. The sound of my violin was nothing more than stilted notes strung together to form a song. Hoon's piano playing was spellbinding. He could hold an audience captive if he so desired, but he chose to play for himself and no one else. Thus, it was Hwan who won the praise of friends and family for his performances of Mozart and Tchaikovsky. Hoon preferred Korean folk songs that spoke to his heart, like the melodic "Arirang," a love ballad about a man's travails as he journeyed through a northern mountain pass.

After trudging through the dark snowy streets, frozen and aching, "Arirang" spoke to me too.

"Ah, little one, there you are!" Hoon exclaimed, relieved to see me. "Why are you so late? I thought you forgot it was Wednesday!"

Exhausted, I wanted to go home and sit by the blazing hearth with a cup of tea while Ajumah fetched me a pail of warm salt water for my sore feet. But I wouldn't miss my once-a-week meal with my favorite brother. Never.

"Sorry I'm late, Hoon. It's my sensei's fault," I said,

choking back tears as I collapsed on a floor cushion next to my brother.

Hoon's face turned dark. He leaned in, worried. "Miyooki? What happened to you?"

"I'll tell you what happened me!" I cried. "I worked at the dye factory all day! I walked four extra miles. Do the math—that's ten miles today. I stood all day at the vats, and I have blisters on my feet. Only children work the dye vats, Hoon. Did you know that? Little children without parents."

Now Hoon was furious. "Those bastards!" he yelled. Curious faces turned our way.

I took off my coat and gloves. "Look at my arms. They're stained blue. Who knows if it will ever come out!"

"Miyooki, you will never go back to that wretched school ever again. Even if I have to strangle your sensei with my own hands!" Hoon vowed through clenched teeth.

I wanted to believe that Hoon could protect me from my cruel sensei. But like all Koreans, he was powerless before the Japanese, no matter how much of a revolutionary he imagined himself to be. Born a rebel at heart, Hoon once spat on his sensei, knowing a severe whipping would inevitably follow. He laughed through the pain as welts rose on his back. Scars formed, but he wore them as proudly as if they were war medals. Still, an army of Hoons was no challenge for the all-powerful Japanese. Not even the Americans could hold their own against the Japanese, I was convinced. It was just a matter of time before Japan took over the world.

There was no avoiding the dye factory tomorrow or the next day. Just the thought of going back to that dark dingy place made me wither like a flower in winter.

"Forget about tomorrow, little one," Hoon said. "Enjoy your meal tonight."

When our warm bowls of noodle soup arrived, I took Hoon's advice and devoured my meal with gusto.

After supper, we sipped traditional *sujeonggwa*—a

cinnamon-sweet after dinner beverage made from persimmons—and I blossomed, the events of the day fading away with my recovery. My stomach was full, and I was in the Udon House with Hoon. Who wouldn't be happy? But I wasn't ready for the walk home just yet. I knew Oma would send me directly to bed where I would fall into a dreamless night of sleep only to wake up for another unbearable day at the dye factory. No, I wanted to go to The Hundred Choices Department Store, even if just to window shop.

"Hoon, please, let's go," I begged him.

He sat for a moment, weighing the consequences. Then, an impish smile crossed his face. "You do know Oma will beat me over the head with a stick for having you out so late."

"Hoon," I whined.

"Ah, little one, it's hard to say no to you."

Icicles hung from the rooftops with luminous effect, making The Hundred Choices Department Store dreamier than it already was. The doors swung open and a gleeful group of young ladies entered, giggling as only the Japanese girls did. Who knew a war was going on? Inside, the tailor was measuring men for suit alterations. Women were gathered around the jewelry and cosmetic counters. We stepped inside, and Hoon was instantly on stage, fawning over his female clientele and, for a moment, I saw shades of Hwan. The difference being that Hoon's performance was worthy of an award.

"Exquisite, Madame Akimoto. Emeralds bring out your lovely eyes," he said smoothly. But I could read his mind: *Madame Akimoto, nothing would bring me more pleasure than to poke out your crinkly Jap eyeballs with the sharpest icicle hanging from The Hundred Choices Department Store!*

I knew my parents were pacing the hall, wondering where I was at this late hour. But tonight, I didn't worry. After my dreadful day, I lavished in the luxury of pearls, red leather gloves, topaz necklaces, gold pins. Possessions which Oma shunned, despite her inherited wealth and majority owner-ship of The Hundred Choices Department Store. She was a God-fearing woman who stood by Apa, the minister of our church. Oma wore her hair in a tight bun, and while some Koreans were adapting to Western-style clothing, she refused, still donning the traditional *hanbok*. Her gaze was never lost in the luster of beautiful things such as the new silk pouches now on display. Her motive was always to lure Hoon away from the streets and into an honest life.

I picked up a pink pouch and ran my fingers over the royal blue embroidered Chinese character symbolizing happiness.

Hoon looked over my shoulder. "They're beautiful, aren't they?"

"Yes," I breathed.

"Would you like one, little one?"

"Yes!" I exclaimed.

3

SOGHA MOUNTAIN

So long Ichiban School! So long hateful sensei! So long dye factory!

Hoon's threat against my sensei was tempered by Apa's own rage, which prompted a shrewd plan that granted me the ultimate wish of every Korean student forced into the Japanese war effort: To skip school.

Forever!

When I arrived home on Hoon's back with bloody, blistered feet and blue-stained arms, Apa banged his fist against the wall and roared, "Enough is enough!"

As a servant of God, Apa was usually a quiet-spoken man. Outbursts were rare. True, he was fluent in five languages, and as a young missionary had traveled the world, spreading the word of God with a powerful message that was heard loud and clear. But he never cursed or spoke poorly of anyone, not even the Japanese. He knew cooperation with the local police was the only way to keep the church open. Even when the police stole church donations, undermining the needs of the hungry, sick, and dying, Apa remained calm. Only once before had I witnessed his anger. On a night fueled by alcohol and bitter words, Hwan and Hoon were at each other's throats about—who else?—the notorious Dai Takagi.

"You hate him because you hate all Japanese!" Hwan accused Hoon between shots of sake. "Dai is a good friend, not to mention a good business partner!"

"I pity you, brother. For only a desperate soul would feel honored to have a Jap for a friend!"

"Look in the mirror, Hoon! You are the definition of a pitiful soul!"

"And you're nothing but a drunk and a traitor!"

Hwan lunged at Hoon, causing both brothers to tumble to the floor. As they wrestled across the parlor, crashing into the wooden table and knocking over Oma's favorite porcelain vase brimming with freshly cut flowers from the garden, Apa burst into the room, appearing larger than life. He was more than twice his sons' age, with silvery-flecked hair, but when pushed, he possessed the strength of Samson. He grabbed Hwan and Hoon by their collars, lifting them off the floor and dragging their bodies to the front door.

"My house is my temple—a place of peace, prayer, and harmony! If you cannot handle your differences like men, then get out!"

My brothers, both stunned and amazed, first by Apa's fury, and secondly by his extraordinary strength, reluctantly shook hands to avoid being tossed to the dark lonely streets.

Apa now held me close and whispered, "No more war effort for you, my little cheonsa."

Yes, the Ichiban School was a thing of the past!

Oma agreed, sipping ginger root tea, her remedy for migraines. "Miyooki, you will stay in Sogha to convalesce from your injuries. Do you understand?"

"Yes, Oma."

Of course, there were no real injuries to speak of, just a few blisters on my feet, which would heal in a week or two. Even my blue-stained arms washed clean the next morning.

So long Ichiban School! So long hateful sensei! So long dye factory!

Even in winter, Sogha mountain was a sanctuary, a gateway to heaven. Our mountain home was surrounded by majestic trees that boasted fruit in the spring and summer months, and fiery leaves in the autumn. They grew persimmons, gingkoes, and chestnuts. Now the trees resembled bare bones against a frozen gray sky. And the mountain retreat was quiet, too quiet for some, but not for me. After the noise of factory machinery and my sensei's constant war effort blather, the silence of snowcapped mountains was music to my ears.

Ajumah accompanied me to Sogha and served as my soul companion on the mountain. She was a small, elderly woman, but with her boundless energy, she made me feel old. Up at the crack of dawn, Ajumah caught fish and chopped wood, went to the market in the valley, washed laundry under the icy waterfall, cooked and cleaned house.

Meanwhile, I slept.

While her hands and face were leathery from a lifetime of labor, her back a little hunched, Ajumah's survival skills were vital to her will and spirit. She suffered from rickets, which made her seem dwarf-like, but her disease never seemed to slow her down no matter how much she rocked side-to-side with each hobbling step. I tried to help with chores, but I only got in her way.

When there was nothing more to do, Ajumah wrote letters, tucking them into a pocket she had sewn inside her *jeogori* jacket closest to her heart. Who the letters were for and whether she ever mailed them was a mystery to me.

Days were utter bliss. I slept in, took long walks on the edge of the cold craggy mountain, collected shiny pebbles and colorful quartz stones along the way, dropping them into the pink silk pouch Hoon had given me. I swung high and low on my wooden swing, suspended from an ancient pine tree overlooking the valley, and gathered frozen chestnuts from the ground. At night, Ajumah and I roasted the chestnuts over a campfire under a starlit sky, sipping warm oolong tea. I did most of the talking, lamenting about how I missed my family, my Wednesday night suppers out with Hoon, and The Hundred Choices Department Store. I talked about the various new arrivals to the store, like the leather Oxfords from London that had nearly caused a stampede, and the limited number of French silk stockings that had young Japanese women lining up hours before the store opened. I could only dream of owning such extravagant accessories. One day, I hinted to Hoon that my thirteenth birthday was just around the corner, never believing in a million years that my wish might come true.

"Oh, Ajumah, when I wore my new Oxfords and French stockings to church the next day, all my friends oohed and aahed! I felt like a princess!"

How spoiled I must have sounded to her.

But on a night full of moon and philosophy, I swore her to secrecy, confessing things I would never share with another soul, not even Hoon. I confided that I questioned my faith in God, that I could not bring myself to believe in Him with the same fervent fire that drove Oma and Apa. Perhaps their blind faith made them better people, but could they truly look around our woeful world and feel God's presence?

"Be honest, Ajumah, do you feel God's presence?"

Ajumah thoughtfully paused, carefully choosing her words. "At times, our world can feel like a cold and hopeless place," she finally spoke. "But whenever you feel like giving up, Miyooki, look to the stars. They will give you hope."

I looked up, gazing. "They're beautiful, but—"

"More than beautiful," Ajumah insisted. "They are tiny sparkles of light passing through time and space just for our human eyes, just to remind us of God's presence, his heaven."

A beautiful thought. I would leave it at that. I wasn't going to challenge Ajumah's beliefs, shatter her hope in a world that already cheated her of a good life.

I told her of Song-ho, the boy at the dye factory, and I cursed this so-called god, the heavens and earth, for his rotten lot in life.

"What will become of him?" I wondered.

"No one knows," Ajumah moaned. "But if he is fortunate,

he will find good people who will change his life for the better as I have done with your family."

"Ajumah, do you really have a better life?"

She nodded. "Yes, Miyooki, I do."

"A *good* life?"

"I think so," she replied.

Like young stars, my admiration for Ajumah was growing more and more with each passing day.

"You like to write letters," I remarked. "They must be for someone very special."

Ajumah winced. "For my grandson."

"Where is he?" I asked her.

"He was recruited into the Japanese Imperial Army earlier this year. I pray for him every night."

I recalled a supper with Hoon when he spoke of the recent Imperial Army recruitment of Korean men—those between the ages of eighteen and twenty-one had been called up first—and how he and Hwan had been lucky to have escaped the draft by a few years.

"A Korean soldier in the Jap Imperial Army is no better than a dead soldier on the front lines," Hoon had said, digging up a fistful of *kalguksu* with his chopsticks.

"My sensei says the Japanese are winning the war," I had said. "Why do they need Korean recruits now?"

Hoon had a good belly laugh. "Your godless sensei is like all Japs—a liar! Don't fall prey to his propaganda. First, the Japs refused Korean participation for fear the training and military position would empower them to revolt against the Imperial Army. Now they are desperate. Why? Because I've told you before, little one, they are losing the war! It is just a matter of time."

Was it true? If so, did that mean Ajumah's grandson was a dead soldier? I could hear Hoon's voice in my head say: "Yes, little one, he is dead!"

"Have you heard from your grandson?" I now asked Ajumah.

She looked to the stars, but they were suddenly blotted out by the moon.

"No," she murmured, gazing hopelessly at the moon the way one does when one aches for the past.

I looked to the moon too.

Most weekends, my parents alternated stays on the mountain. And when Hoon could sneak away from the department store, he would surprise me with the occasional visit. Apa caught me up on my reading and math skills as well as my Bible studies. He introduced me to Korean history—the wars that were fought, the great kings and queens that lived, the opulent dynasties that had ruled for centuries. How tragic it was that I knew so little about my own country and people. But who could blame me? My parents seldom spoke of Korea and, prior to the war effort, I was too brainwashed by the Japanese to even ask. So why were my parents talking about it now?

"Japan is losing the war," Apa said.

Japan is losing the war. Sometimes I wondered if my sensei and Principal Shimmura were skeptical of my "injuries" and the time I needed to convalesce. If so, they never voiced their suspicions, at least that I was aware of. Or maybe it was because Japan really was losing the war, and they had more important things on their minds.

"Ha!" Hoon laughed one evening as we sat by the hearth playing cards. "The weekly sack of rice and basket of eggs Apa delivers to their doorsteps keep their Jap mouths shut!"

4

A MIRACLE ON SOGHA MOUNTAIN

Small gestures are never forgotten...

While my weekdays were spent in joyful solitude, one Saturday morning Oma asked me to accompany her to the orphanage in the valley. I tagged along with half-hearted enthusiasm, though curious to meet the newest group of children who had stolen Oma's heart.

"Helping others in need is the best education," Oma said.

These days, the definition of a good education eluded me as well as the benefits associated with it. When we arrived at the orphanage, all the children rushed toward Oma, gathering around her with loving hugs and kisses, overwhelming me with emotion. Their eyes reminded me of Song-ho's, hollow and sad. Every tiny face haunted me, making me want to protect their poor souls. But my role was limited to reading Bible stories, preparing meals, and organizing games—trivial activities that couldn't change their lives.

"You are wrong, Miyooki," Oma said. "You bring smiles to their faces, a little sunshine to their lives. Small gestures are never forgotten."

And so I reserved my weekends for the orphans—Song-ho always on my mind, hoping my rice ball and lemon candies had given him a reason to believe that not all people were as evil as Mr. Lee, the dye factory supervisor.

In the evenings, I revisited my Chuseok moon. By the light of a lantern, I worked on the project, one stitch up, one stitch down, filling in the moon. Sometimes Ajumah would look over my shoulder, quietly observing, grunting with approval. When the moon was done, I beamed with pride. It was far from perfect, but despite the few frayed threads and uneven stitches here and there, Ajumah insisted my moon was beautiful. I wanted to believe her, but when I stood back and observed for myself, all I saw was any old moon suspended in one-dimensional space. Where was the poetry, the haiku on canvas?

"Ajumah, my moon looks lonely," I declared.

"Why not create a Chuseok scene?" she suggested. "Tell a story, something meaningful."

Tell a story, something meaningful. An ingenious idea, but how could I create a Chuseok scene without art in my bones? Even though I'd earned As in art class, grades had been based on effort and completion rather than talent. After all, Koreans were a gift-less people, at least that's what my sensei used to tell us. Puh! Apa taught me that Korean art dated back to the Neolithic Age, and Hwan and Hoon were living proof of my sensei's lies. From their musicality to their artful design of The Hundred Choices Department Store, they weren't coined the Masterful Twins in the Korean community for nothing. Unlike my brothers' many talents, however, I was limited to my athletic prowess, which had won me blue ribbons in the rope climbing, broad jump, and hundred-yard dash contests at school. Yes, I could run faster than any boy my age, but running and jumping wouldn't be of much use for my art project. And so, night after night, I stared blankly at my canvas. Sometimes, my mind wandered back to my home, Sinuiju, a place that was growing mythical in my mind. To keep my hometown alive in my heart, I thought constantly of family, Wednesday night suppers out with Hoon, and The Hundred Choices Department Store. My sadness only deepened as I yearned for all of those familiar things. But whenever I thought about the Ichiban School or the dye factory, I was grateful to be in Sogha, however lonesome it could be.

"I can't think of a story or anything meaningful," I told Ajumah one night.

"Don't worry, Miyooki. It will come to you when you least expect it."

❧

Winter's silence was replaced by the sound of rushing rivers and creeks and baby birds chirping in their nests. Bright azaleas and golden forsythia lit up the mountainside in glorious renewal. Now that the weather was milder, the orphans were out and about picking flowers, hiking, and learning agricultural skills such as hoeing and planting. I loved the changing seasons, the delicate cherry blossoms of spring, the lotus ponds in summer. But I was growing painfully homesick, missing Sinuiju, the lights, the energy that only my city could offer. And once the monsoon rains arrived in July, life on the mountain ceased to exist. For three long weeks, I was holed up in the house with nothing to do. Not even Oma and Apa visited on weekends, given the threat of mudslides below us. Ajumah tried her best to entertain me with a daily marathon of *Paduk*, a board game played with shiny black and white stones in which opponents try to capture territories. One game could last for hours or be over in a minute, depending on a player's strategy. Of course, Ajumah beat me hands down every time. We made *mandoo* dumplings and *jijim* pancakes. At night while Ajumah wrote letters, I took out my lonely moon on canvas, trying my best to visualize a meaningful Chuseok scene to no avail. Why was it so difficult? Where was the inspiration?

At last, the monsoon rains ended, and the clouds parted to reveal a magnificent blue sky. I stepped outside and reveled in the hot sun on my face. Then, I raced down the mountainside, mud splashing at my ankles. I stood beneath the rushing waterfall and smelled the earthy air. I picked wildflowers for the orphans and surprised them with a visit. They formed a happy circle around me, jumping up and down, basking in the sun. I thought about Song-ho, wondering if he'd ever felt the sun on his face, if he'd ever experienced a moment like this. It was hard to imagine.

When I returned home, I took the path through the gardens, sniffing fragrant fruit dangling from the persimmon trees, thinking how utterly blissful the world was, at least on this quiet mountaintop with its magnificent sunset view. I could gaze out at it forever, in awe of a sky no artist could recreate and no human could mar.

And then it happened...

Yes, just as Ajumah had said—when I least expected it, a vision would come to me. And she was right. A beautiful Chuseok scene came to life in full color. I rushed inside the house and went straight to work transferring the image in my head onto my canvas.

On that same day, something far more magnificent occurred: Japan's World War II surrender. You could hear the bell of freedom ringing from distant villages. I wondered with glee if my sensei was bawling his beady eyes out. *We are winning the war against the American devil.* Puh, again! Lies, lies, all lies! I couldn't wait to go home, back to the Udon House with Hoon, back to The Hundred Choices Department Store where I could smell perfume in the air. I couldn't wait to run through the streets of Sinuiju and cry—*FREEDOM!*

But something was wrong. Ajumah seemed worried, and yet, she went about her day doing chores as if nothing had happened. And where were my parents? Why had they not come for me?

"They will keep their weekend schedule," Ajumah said, hunched over a large tub of spring water, rinsing mountain roots.

"But why? The war is over, and Korea is free! Everything has changed! We can go home! Why aren't we celebrating? Ajumah, aren't you happy?"

Ajumah tasted a root to ensure its crunchy texture, chewing with the few teeth that remained in her mouth. "Miyooki, change is not always good."

"It is if it means we are free," I said.

"Not when thousands of civilian lives were sacrificed."

I frowned. "Ajumah, what do you mean?"

"When I was at the market this morning, the villagers were saying that Americans bombed two Japanese cities in the past few days. They said the bombs destroyed both cities. Countless innocent men, women, and children lost their lives. Who knows, Korea could be next."

Was it true? I didn't know what to think or feel or even believe. On Sogha, we were cloistered from the outside world. Nothing was real, but the mountains and sky and the valley below, which were peaceful and majestic that day as they had been the day before and on the days bombs had supposedly dropped over Japan.

"How could a bomb destroy a whole city?" I asked, skeptical.

"I don't know," Ajumah said. "I'm just telling you what I heard, but I think it is true. Why else would Japan surrender?"

If those rumors were true, I wasn't going to feel bad about it. It was fate, it seemed. After all, Hoon had told me that the Japanese bombing of Pearl Harbor had started the war with America in the first place. How many lives had Japan taken in their quest to take over all of Asia? How many Koreans had they enslaved and forced into *their* ugly war?

"Well, I don't believe the Americans would bomb Korea. Let's face it, Ajumah, the Japanese are to blame for the death and destruction in their own country!" I blurted, suddenly shocked by my own hateful words.

Ajumah was too. "Miyooki," she murmured, aghast.

"I'm sorry," I said, ashamed. "I didn't mean what I said."

I was quickly learning that war brought out the worst in everyone—my sensei, Mr. Lee, and, yes, even me.

"I know you didn't mean it," Ajumah said. "But you should know, even if the Americans don't bomb Korea, word comes that there is trouble in Sinuiju."

I panicked, worrying about my family. "Trouble? What kind of trouble?"

"Russian soldiers are policing the streets."

"Why would they do that?"

"To protect us from the Americans."

I was confused. "But the Americans won the war and gave us freedom from the Japanese," I said. "They're not our enemy, they're our friends."

"Apparently, the Russians don't see things our way," Ajumah said. "At least that is what the villagers are saying."

"What about my family? Are they okay?"

"Your oma sent a messenger," Ajumah said. "They are fine. But as you know, your apa speaks fluent Russian. He overheard Russian officers talking about the power struggles with the Americans in the South."

"Does this mean another war?" I wondered.

"I don't know, Miyooki. No one knows."

When my parents arrived on the weekend, they confirmed my worst fear: I wasn't going home.

"Is it because of the Russian soldiers?" I asked Apa.

"Yes, Miyooki, there is much unrest and rioting in Sinuiju. When there is peace and harmony, you will return home."

"Does this mean all of you will be coming here?"

"No, Miyooki," Apa said. "We will remain in Sinuiju and go about our business for now."

"But, Apa, why are there Russian soldiers in Sinuiju? Ajumah heard they are policing the streets, protecting us from the Americans. Is this true?"

"They claim to be here to protect our land, but for whom remains the question."

Freedom had been short lived, Apa explained, when

Russian forces rapidly moved into the northern region like a flood of chaos. Japanese residents were terrified to leave their homes, locking their doors and hiding in closets. Koreans were no better off, walking through the streets of Sinuiju with fear and trepidation. So I stayed on Sogha mountain, waiting for the world to find peace and harmony.

Autumn swept into Sogha, with falling leaves and cold winds, and the arrival of family to the mountain for a Chuseok celebration. Ajumah and I had spent the morning making *yakgwa*, flower-shaped honey cookies garnished with a trio of pine nuts, traditionally served during the holiday. The delicious smell of dough frying in oil made my mouth water. When I greeted Oma with her favorite sweet treat, her eyes brightened. If she had a migraine, it lifted at least for a moment as she plucked a cookie from the plate. Not even Ajumah's prized *gimbap*, the Korean version of sushi, could whet Oma's appetite. But yakgwa was the exception, for Oma could devour a dozen cookies and still hunger for more.

"Exquisite," she sighed, eyes closed as if in prayer. "Heaven on earth."

And now my full Chuseok moon hung on the wall behind the buffet table covered with holiday fare—a variety of *panchon* vegetable dishes, seasoned *dubu* (better known in the West as tofu), mountain grown mushrooms, mandoo dumplings, spicy *kimchi* cabbage pancakes, yakgwa, and more. No longer a lonely moon, my Chuseok moon's halo of light glowed over a little boy in the image of Song-ho, picking fruit from a persimmon tree. This was the life I wished for the boy trapped in Hell's Chamber. Like my silk pouch, I stitched the symbol of happiness into the lower right corner of my haiku on canvas. Surely my sensei would mark my project with a bold *F* for its Korean-ness, but the praise of loved ones made me beam with pride.

"Beautiful!"

"Enchanting!"

"Wonderful!"

"Lovely!"

Like all Chuseoks of the past, we hiked up the mountain-side to the burial grounds of our ancestors and prayed. We sang songs and danced circles around their graves, for the three-day harvest holiday was a joyful event to honor long lost loved ones. We made half-moon rice cakes filled with creamy yellow mung bean paste, sliced luscious persimmons, and roasted sweet potatoes. Even Hwan and Hoon were in festive moods, playing Korean chess called *Janggi*, with Hoon winning nine times out of ten. Together, they competed in the annual kite-fighting contest in the valley and took first prize. At night under the full Chuseok moon, we sat around a blazing campfire, sipping *boricha* tea and nibbling walnut tea cakes. But this Chuseok night, conversation revolved around the Russian presence in the north, and the uncertainty that hung in the autumn air.

"How long will they be here?" my aunt Imo wondered.

"A temporary state," my uncle Samchon insisted.

Hoon argued. "The Soviets in the north and Americans in the south. I see a bloody civil war coming."

"Rubbish," Hwan retorted. "Once we establish our own government, the world powers will leave the country."

Hoon shook his head. "Brother, for a history and anthropology major, you are either naïve or you learned nothing in school."

Apa interjected before a fight could start. "All we can do is wait and see," he said. "Now let's enjoy the Chuseok moon."

Had we known this would be our final Chuseok holiday together, we would never have stopped gazing at the moon.

5

RUSSIAN SOLDIERS

Our eyes locked before the train left the station...

On a blustery Thursday afternoon in October, my parents arrived at the mountain home, unannounced. Ajumah and I were busy filling giant *onggi* clay pots with kimchi, which would be buried in the ground over the long winter, while singing "Santoki," an old children's song. Apa went directly to the safe and removed its contents—money, jewels, watches—and placed them into a leather knapsack.

"Apa, what are you doing?" I asked.

"Quickly," Oma said to both Ajumah and me. "We must pack our clothes and catch the next train back to Sinuiju."

The urgency in her voice put panic in my heart. But I didn't ask questions for fear her answers would terrify me. As Oma requested, I packed up my belongings, carefully folding and placing my full Chuseok moon in my suitcase.

After Apa locked up the house, we embarked down the mountain, hushed in our own thoughts. The silence held a pall over the mountainside. Even if it were nighttime and the sky bursting with stars, they would fail to give me hope. Like gazing at the Chuseok moon, had I known this would be our last visit to Sogha mountain, I would never have let my family leave.

Before boarding the train, Apa gave the leather knapsack of valuables to Oma. He then turned to me, firmly squeezing my shoulders—a gesture saved for crises like Oma's grave illness with hepatitis two winters earlier. Then, I had feared life would never be the same. But Oma healed, defying the odds.

Everything is going to be okay, I now told myself over and over. *Everything is going to be okay*. Did I believe my own words?

"Miyooki, listen carefully. There is political unrest in Sinuiju. Armed Russian soldiers are guarding the streets. On your way home with Oma and Ajumah, please keep to yourself and do not make eye contact with the soldiers. They are potentially dangerous. Once home, you will remain inside at all times, never leaving our compound. Is that understood?"

"But, Apa, you are coming with us, right?"

Apa bit his quivering lip and held me close to his chest. His voice wavered. "Miyooki, you will always be my little cheonsa. But I must stay here."

"Why, Apa, why?" I said, growing hysterical.

"As a minister, I am a threat to the emerging government, and it is too dangerous for me to return to Sinuiju. I not only endanger my own life, but more importantly, the lives of my family. Now board the train and stay close to Oma and Ajumah."

"What do you mean the emerging government? Are the Russians taking over our country?"

"No one can answer that question right now," he said. "Things are changing fast in Korea."

"Apa, is there going to be a civil war?"

"I hope not, Miyooki. Now, please, board the train."

"But where are you staying? At the summer house?"

Apa shook his head. "Friends of the church have found a place for me to stay."

"Where?"

"Miyooki, I cannot disclose the location, it is too dangerous for you to know."

"Apa..." I murmured. "When will I see you again? Why is this happening?"

"It is a temporary separation," he said, trying to reassure both of us. "Hopefully, we will be together again soon, when order is restored. Until then, you must stay calm and do as your oma and I say."

I clutched Apa with white knuckles, not wanting to let go, but he gently nudged me away and into Oma's arms. My parents briefly hugged before Oma quickly ushered me onto the train. I took my seat and pressed my hands against the window, watching Apa. Our eyes locked before the train left the station.

"Goodbye, Apa," I whispered as he grew smaller and smaller.

As the train slowly moved along the tracks, I couldn't help but wonder why we were heading to Sinuiju now, into a firestorm of chaos. Why couldn't we stay in the countryside with Apa?

"It is just a matter of time before the Red Army finds their way to the countryside," Oma said. "We must go about our lives in Sinuiju and blend in with the community."

"But what about Apa?"

"He is safe for now," she said. "The Russians will not find him."

"But what if they come looking for him?"

"If they come to our door asking about his whereabouts, we do not have to lie, because we do not know. But I must warn you, Miyooki, the city has been destroyed by looters. The Hundred Choices Department Store was burned to the ground."

"No!" I wailed. "Who would do such a thing? It was the Russians, wasn't it?"

"There is no time for pointing fingers," Oma said. "What's done is done."

"But why would they set fire to our store?"

"Many establishments were burned to the ground, Miyooki, not just ours. The city is in ruins."

Suddenly I wanted to step back in time, back to Sogha, where I could hear the monsoon rains hit our rooftop while playing endless games of Paduk with Ajumah. Clutching my silk pouch, I twirled the tassel with my finger, happiness gone.

I turned to Oma whose eyes were now closed in prayer, her tired face telling a story of sleepless nights. Ajumah looked straight ahead, her face ghostly pale. Was she thinking about her grandson? I gazed out the window to a picturesque fall day. It was hard to believe Russian soldiers were just beyond the painted mountains, poisoning my beloved city of Sinuiju.

When we arrived in Sinuiju, I stepped off the train to a heart-breaking sight—rows of looted shops closed for business. Most, as Oma said, had been burned to the ground. Yes, the Duk Jip and the Udon House, and most tragically The Hundred Choices Department Store. Oma tried to warn me, but nothing could have prepared me for the wreckage before my eyes. I gasped. The once beautiful shop was swept of life. All that remained was shattered glass, remnants of broken jewelry cases, beheaded mannequins, and mounds of ash. I tried not to make eye contact with the bedraggled white men and women who paced back and forth on street corners, holding brown loaves of bread under their arms and giant machine guns over their shoulders, but it was hard to ignore their glares. I presumed they were the Russian soldiers, but they didn't look like any soldiers I had ever seen before. They reminded me of the Russian beggars Hwan called gypsies who emigrated to Korea only to live on the streets, dirty and homeless, a look of bewilderment in their eyes. Apa's church had opened its doors to the throngs of poor gypsy souls who were unarmed and harmless, unlike the savages who now stood guard, pointing their guns at passersby and spitting on the pavement.

"Oma—" I murmured, crushed.

"Shh, we will talk later," she said as we walked home through the once vibrant city now grayer than the smoke that used to pipe into the air from the chimneys of the now-abandoned dye factory.

"Were those men and women the Russian soldiers?" I asked her.

"Yes, but boys and girls forced to be adults," she said, shaking her head. "They belong at home with their families. Their daily food stipend consists of a single loaf of bread."

"They don't look like boys and girls to me," Ajumah said.

I agreed, observing some soldiers donning rows of designer watches from wrist to elbow, surely stolen from The Hundred Choices Department Store!

"Oma, they look evil."

A military vehicle slowly drove by us with uniformed men aboard. Like the soldiers, the men were white, armed, and possessed an air of intimidation. As the vehicle passed through the intersection, the soldiers saluted the men in uniform and were, in turn, acknowledged with slow, superior nods.

"Who are they?" I asked Oma.

"Russian officers," she replied.

Once home, I left all fear of Russian soldiers outside the stone wall of our compound. Indeed, the looted streets of Sinuiju were forgotten to the beauty of home, which remained unscathed by war and politics. My brothers were in the parlor, deep in sober conversation concerning the leftover inventory from the department store. Hwan smoked a cigarette, a habit he usually reserved for outside the house away from our parents. I had never seen him so glum. Gone was the confidence, the poise of a worldly man. He ran a hand through his unkempt hair as Hoon spoke.

"It's about surviving the bloody Russian invasion, Hwan. Nothing more. Forget about the store. It's gone. And for god's sake, forget about Dai. Another war is coming."

Hwan looked down at the floor, shoulders slumped as if giving up entirely would be easier than surviving in our new world devoid of dreams, hopes, and Dai Takagi. When I entered the room, all talk of our grim reality ceased. My brothers leapt to their feet to greet me.

"Miyooki!" they exclaimed, huddling around me.

My brothers put on a good act with pained smiles, trying their best to shield me from the cold, cruel world that was now Sinuiju. But I had already left Apa at the train station. I had seen the Russian soldiers and witnessed their barbaric behavior. I had seen what was left of The Hundred Choices Department Store. And even though I felt safe at home, protected by my two strapping brothers and a giant stone wall, when I stood on the *daecheong*, I could still hear the savages—their foreign tongues, their evil laughter, their gunfire. I didn't know these men and women, but I hated them anyway.

That evening, we all sat down to a meal. Typically, the morning meal had always been the main event of the day, the only meal that brought us all together for prayer, good food, and laughter before going our separate ways. I had always been the first to leave the table, and my family's sendoffs—"Have a good day, Miyooki! Bye, bye, little one!"—always left me with an empty feeling, one of deep sadness and dread for the day ahead at the Ichiban School. Our busy schedules—school for me, Oma with her orphans, Apa swamped with church activities, Hoon overseeing the department store, and Hwan, well, he was hardly ever around—made it impossible to sit down to any other meals together.

Hwan's mysterious whereabouts always left a hole in Oma's heart. I loved my big brother the way all little sisters do, but the truth was, he was too busy chasing dreams, making deals, and living the life of a perpetual bachelor to spend much time with me. Yes, he was the dashing brother who belonged to the world, the brother who adored beautiful Japanese girls donning kimonos, which made Oma cringe.

"When will you find a nice Korean girl and settle down?" she'd once asked him.

"Oma, when a nice Korean girl feels like silk and smells of jasmine."

And while brother Hoon broke Oma's heart too, he was my soulmate. True, he was a loner, the defiant one who refused to eat Japanese-style noodles, opting for the Korean kalguksu at the Udon House. And true, again, Hoon only loved our family and no one else, but that made me the lucky recipient of all his affection.

So here we were, seated around the supper table, each of us missing Apa in our own cherished ways: he was Oma's loving companion, Hwan and Hoon's wise peacemaker, and my hero.

How I longed for the past, for a morning meal with Apa, for his ritual prayer that always included a little humor to get a poignant thought across. "We are grateful for the food before us, including the seasoned watercress that my children choose not to eat even though they know this vitamin and mineral rich cruciferous vegetable is quite healthy for them, good for their hearts and digestion. Pardon my digression, Lord, but you understand. Now where was I? Oh yes, dear Lord, we have not forgotten your words—'Behold, I have given you every plant yielding seed that is on the face of all the earth, and every tree with seed in its fruit. You shall have them for food.' Thank you, Lord. Amen."

Now, we had only a meager supper set before us, one artfully displayed thanks to Ajumah: Seasoned mountain roots called *doraji*, yellow sweet potatoes, and red bean-flecked rice. I sat between my brothers, head down, eyes closed, holding my hands in prayer.

"Hoon," Oma said, nudging him to begin the prayer.

Hoon cleared his throat, pondering his words. And though prayer was not his poetry, when he finally spoke, I grew emotional, knowing Apa would be proud.

"Dear Lord, as you know, this is not the voice that you normally hear at our table, but our beloved apa is not here."

Painful pause.

"We pray that you provide him food and shelter and guide him to safety in these troubling times."

"Amen," we uttered.

"And dear Lord," Hoon continued, "thank you for this meal…"

As my brother continued the supper prayer, I opened my eyes and glanced around the table at my family. Although this was a peaceful break from the madness of the day, Apa's empty seat was a grim reminder that our world was crumbling around us.

After supper, Ajumah and I unpacked my belongings, taking our time, savoring our first private moment since leaving Sogha so abruptly that afternoon. It was hard to believe just hours ago we had been on the mountain, jarring kimchi and humming songs. So much had happened between then and now.

"Ajumah, do you think a civil war is coming?" I asked her.

"I can only hope not," she said, meticulously smoothing out all my garments and hanging them in the closet. "But if there is a war, we will survive."

"How do you know we'll survive? Do you really believe your grandson is ever coming home? Do you really think he survived the war?"

Ajumah's face grew dark. "I have no choice but to believe and have faith, Miyooki. Otherwise, I have lost everything."

"I want to believe too. But I don't even recognize my own city anymore. The Hundred Choices Department Store was burned to the ground. Apa is gone and I don't even know where he is or when I'll see him again. And Russian soldiers are policing our streets. Ajumah, it's hard for me to have faith."

"Miyooki, let us not concentrate on things we have no control over. Your room needs some love and attention. Now where would you like to hang your Chuseok moon?"

Ajumah's unwavering optimism never ceased to amaze me. How could she remain hopeful when her own grandson was never coming home? When our beautiful city was up in smoke, torched by foreigners? I was learning that hard lives built survivors who would always rise above the ashes.

I looked out the window with Song-ho on my mind. Now that the dye factory had closed, where had he gone? Was he even alive? I shuddered, thinking the worst. Taking Ajumah's advice, I turned to my room. Better to focus on things I could control in this world and not on the sinister acts of outsiders. I stood in the middle of the room, observing each wall with *feng shui* harmony in mind, honoring the principles of peace and happiness. I decided the wall directly in front of my bedding made the most sense, offering the maximum positive *chi* or energy upon rising and falling asleep.

Later in the evening, Hwan and Hoon climbed into the attic above my parents' quarters. I was curious, but not enough to follow them into a space where mice often scurried about.

I heard footsteps and rummaging overhead.

What were my brothers doing up there? Soon they emerged, tossing down a variety of garments, specifically winter wear. Coats, wool socks, thermal underwear, gloves, blankets—the less glamorous offerings of The Hundred Choices Department Store.

"What's going on?" I asked them.

They made their way down the ladder, grabbed the clothes, and rushed by in a blur, oblivious to me.

"What's going on?" I repeated, chasing them into the parlor where Oma was waiting.

No reply.

Oma and Hwan began folding the clothes into a large burlap sack as Hoon tallied numbers on his abacus, the same black and white calculating tool from his former office at The Hundred Choices Department Store.

"Fifteen-hundred *won*," he said.

My family was too preoccupied to be bothered with my questions or even aware, it seemed, of my presence in the room. So I left, retreating to my parents' quarters. There, I climbed the ladder, poking my head inside the attic—expecting an unpleasant encounter with rodents, bats, and other creepy, crawly creatures—in search of answers. To my utter shock and delight my eyes fell upon a glorious sight: A clean and well-lit space with rows and rows of winter coats, sweaters, and thermal underwear among many other items hanging on clothes racks from The Hundred Choices Department Store. Why was all this neatly inventoried merchandise stowed away in the attic? And where were the precious jewels and fine suits, the pearl pins and silk scarves, the perfume and cologne? I knew where the eighteen-karat gold watches were—embellishing the filthy arms of foreign soldiers!

I ran back toward the parlor just as Hoon was leaving the house, tossing the burlap sack over his shoulder on his way out. Pausing at the front gate, he was clearly on the lookout for someone. I sat on the daecheong and peered out the window, observing as a clandestine meeting unfolded: A shadowy figure appeared at the gate, handed over a fistful of money for the burlap sack, and then vanished into the night. Hoon, then, quickly retreated to the house.

"Who was that man?" I asked Hoon, following him into the parlor where Hwan and Oma anxiously awaited. "Was he a customer from the department store?"

Hoon howled with laughter. "Any Japs who are still in Korea are in hiding, little one. They are hated by everyone—the Russians, the Koreans, all of us."

Hwan's face sagged. "Sad but true, Miyooki."

"For most Koreans, it is poetic justice," Hoon stated.

"Hush," Oma said, silencing my brothers before a fight could break out. After all, Apa wasn't there to intervene.

"Then who was that man at the gate?" I wondered.

"Mr. Lim," Oma informed me.

"Mr. Lim from the Duk Jip?"

Oma nodded. "Cold weather is coming, and there is a

high demand for winter clothing. We are selling what is left of our inventory to friends of the community. Fortunately, we are selling the clothes for a reasonable price and making enough to survive on."

"But for how long?" Hoon said, worried. "Our fate is in the hands of the two world powers."

Hwan agreed. "Winter is only so long, and we can only sell so many coats and hats."

Oma sighed, rubbing her aching temples.

First the Japanese, now the Russians. Who or what was next? No one knew.

6

DAI TAKAGI

I hardly recognized the once debonair young man now clad in black peasant clothing...

My only glimpse of the outside world came while observing Hoon's private meetings at the front gate. One by one Korean members of the church and community appeared like phantoms in the night, eluding soldiers, to purchase their coats and other accessories for the looming winter. The Lees, the Pangs, the Kims, the Baks, the Hongs, the Chungs. They were all friends who had never stepped foot inside The Hundred Choices Department Store, well-aware of the unspoken law of the land: Establishments that catered to the Japanese did not cater to Koreans. There was no ill will towards my family, however, as Oma and Apa had not only donated all their time to the church and community, but large sums from their department store earnings as well.

One evening an unexpected guest arrived at the front gate. Snow was falling, and the world was hushed and peaceful. On a night like this, it seemed that no evil existed, and no blood stained the streets of Sinuiju. And yet, I had overheard my brothers telling Oma of the brutality they had witnessed beyond the stone wall of our home more than a few times. Now the Red Army was growing increasingly antagonistic towards rebellious Koreans or those suspected of Christian beliefs. Oddly, the community church remained unscathed, and no Russian soldier dared to enter its premises.

"They killed an innocent man just because he stood outside of a church!" Hwan had said.

"Shot dead before our very eyes!" Hoon added. "Oma, you need to avoid the church. It is a death trap now!"

But Oma would not be deterred. Every morning she went to church, head held high as she passed armed soldiers. Like the highly infectious lepers she bravely nursed in the caves in the countryside, I suspected she was not afraid of any Russian soldier. Yes, if they were to beat or kill her, so be it. Oma would die, proudly, serving God. Curiously, the soldiers let her be, allowing her to come and go as she pleased. Maybe it was Oma's saintly aura that kept the soldiers at bay.

"Or more likely the bags of baked goods she gives those rotten scavengers every day!" Hoon suggested.

Still, I worried. I was forbidden to go anywhere, but every morning and night, Oma walked through a danger zone, a minefield of violence on her way to and from the church and orphanage. I was bewildered. Why would she risk her life, especially when Apa's whereabouts were unknown? Early on, we were hopeful the separation would be temporary, but the Red Army's roundup of church ministers for "interrogation" made any imminent reunion unlikely.

"They're rounding them up like cattle," Hwan said.

"Never to be seen again, buried in mass graves," Hoon lamented.

There was even talk of a new Korean leader on the horizon, an enigmatic figure who had been exiled from the country during the Japanese reign. Now he was poised to return, to take back our country.

"Or destroy it," Hoon said.

But tonight, all of that seemed far away as I gazed outside at tender snowflakes drifting against a pitch-black sky.

This time it was Hwan who went to the gate with buoyant footsteps to greet his old friend Dai Takagi. Hoon, chewing on a toothpick, looked on with hostile eyes. I hardly recognized the once debonair young man, now clad in black peasant clothing. He was a shell of his former self, a hunched, slight man with eyes as sunken as his spirit. Gone was the brashness of wealth and youth, of Japanese blood.

Hoon shook his head without a speck of compassion for the man. "Why do you bring this greedy monger to our house?" he asked Hwan. "Surely, he is here for *his* share of the profits. Or, Dai, do you come bearing gifts for us poor, pitiful Koreans you stole from?"

"Quiet," Oma said, turning her attention to Dai with merciful eyes. "How is your family?"

Dai fell to his knees in despair, now at eye-level with Ajumah who was on all fours cleaning the ondal floors. "We have no food or money. We hide in our home, desperate and hungry, which is why I am here. We have lost everything."

"Everything?" Hoon said, disgusted. "What about all the valuable jewels you smuggled from the department store, leaving us with nothing but coats and underwear?"

Dai dropped his head, ashamed of his actions. "Gone in a night," he replied. "Japanese people are instant targets of the Red Army. They broke down our door and took everything but our lives and the clothes on our backs."

"You poor, pitiful Japanese man," Hoon scoffed. "You cared nothing for our welfare and now you show up at our doorstep pleading for help?"

"Leave him alone!" Hwan spoke up. "Where is your humanity, Hoon? Have Oma and Apa taught you nothing?"

"They taught me to survive the greedy thievery of this man who took everything from us! Why do you defend him, Hwan?"

Oma stood before Hoon. "We are children of God," she said. "We do not turn away those in need. His family should not be punished for his sins."

Hoon observed in shock and disbelief as Oma crossed the room and removed a wad of money from a drawer and placed it in Dai's hands.

"Oma!" he cried. "Have you gone mad?"

"Shh!" Oma hushed him. "Someday, Hoon, the anger in your heart will heal and you will embrace all people, not just Koreans."

Dai began to wail baby tears, bowing profusely before Oma like a worshipper at a shrine. "Thank you, thank you, thank you…" he said over and over. It was hard to watch a grown man cry like a child. Oma raised Dai's chin and spoke.

"Live your life with a pure heart, and that is all the thanks we need."

Dai wiped the tears from his cheeks and rose from the floor. He turned to leave, then paused, looking over his shoulder at Hoon. "I'm truly sorry for everything I have done to you and your family. And I apologize for not treating you with the honor and respect you deserve. Hoon, you were a great manager, the heart and soul of The Hundred Choices Department Store."

Then Dai and Hwan left the house, a twosome morphing into shadows under the soft guise of peaceful falling snow.

7

BLOODSHED

Blood puddles formed, paralyzing me with horror…

Hoon was in a fury, outraged first by Hwan who brought Dai
to our home, and secondly by Oma who had given away his
hard-earned money to a "dirty Jap."

"You took from your own family to spare the life of an
evil man, a dirty Jap no less!" Hoon cried.

"Dai is not evil," Oma insisted. "He is just misguided."

"Oma, wherever you walk, there is good and evil, even
your precious Bible says so. And Dai is evil, no different than
the dirty Jap policemen who murdered Ajumah's husband!
If the tables were turned, do you think he would offer us a
red cent? No! He would take our last grains of rice to save
himself."

Did Hoon speak the truth? Had Ajumah's husband been
murdered at the hands of the Japanese police? She looked up
from the floor, our eyes met, and I knew the answer.

"No!" Hwan shouted. "Dai is not a murderer! You put
up walls and never gave him a chance, which is why he
never talked to you. You hate the world, because you never
amounted to anything. You were a street boy when Dai suggested you manage the department store. No, it wasn't me or
Oma or Apa who gave you the job. We had our reservations,
but Dai said 'Give Hoon a chance. He is your brother, after
all.' And this is how you repay him?"

"Hwan," Oma spoke up, "do not defend Dai with lies."

"Brother, you are blinded or completely brainwashed by
the Japanese!" Hoon said. "Dai simply wanted me around to

have another Korean to spit on! He took every valuable piece of merchandise from the department store. And did you not see him walk out of here with a pocketful of money? Quit defending the enemy, you fool."

"I'm not the fool, Hoon. As I've said a hundred times before, look in the mirror and you will see a fool!"

"No, *you* look in the mirror, brother! I know it's painful to see a Korean man looking back at you, but the truth is, no matter how hard you try to convince yourself otherwise, you will never be Japanese!"

"And you will always be a miserable Korean man!" Hwan said.

Apa always played the peacemaker between my quarreling brothers, but now that he was gone, Oma took the reins with a controlled approach.

"Stop," she said in the calmest of voices. "If you both looked in the mirror, you would see nothing but ugliness looking back at you."

Hoon was fed up with his family, with Oma's devout heart, and with the world. He grabbed his coat and swiftly left the house.

I chased after him, crying out his name. "Hoon, come back!"

But he ignored my plea, exiting the compound and vanishing into the night. I ran to the stone wall and opened the gate, looking down both ends of the street. No sign of him anywhere. Just as I stepped outside, Hwan grabbed my arm.

"Leave him be, Miyooki," he said. "You are only following trouble."

I pushed Hwan away. "*You* are the trouble in this family!" I cried, fire in my veins. "You care more about your Japanese friend than you do us! How could you say such hateful things to Hoon? He is your blood brother! Why do you torture him so?"

"Miyooki, you are just an innocent young girl," Hwan

said, trying his best to stay calm. "Hoon is the one with hate in his heart, not me. He blames Dai and the whole Japanese race for his own failings. I accept what is and make the best of circumstances. It's called survival."

"If survival means giving up your dignity and putting friends before family, then I would rather die!"

Now Hwan erupted in anger. "You are starting to sound like Hoon, a failure! All talk, talk, talk, a 'Korean patriot' without a cause, without a real fight in you!"

"I'm a proud Korean, Hwan, not someone who lives in shame like you do!" I lashed back. "And stop calling Hoon a failure! Without him, The Hundred Choices Department Store would have gone under a long time ago. You never stopped in long enough to see how hard he worked or how much his employees loved him. Even his Japanese customers loved him. But how would you know? You were too busy pretending you were one of *them*! Well, you're not Japanese, Hwan. You're Korean! Korean! Do you hear me?"

Suddenly, and like thunder, a piercing cry cracked the sky ending our shouting match. I peered outside the gate, horrified, witnessing the first in a series of violent acts that would taint my view of the world: A Russian soldier pistol-whipping an old woman over the head, his armed comrade laughing as he looks on. A helpless young boy—likely a grandson—stands by in horror as the soldier throws the woman to the ground, kicking her writhing body.

What happened next was a surreal Godsend or a nightmare, depending on where you stood: A Red Army military vehicle appeared out of nowhere, stopping at the scene long enough for a Russian officer to raise his weapon and pull the trigger. In a loud, violent flash of bullets, the soldiers went down, one lifeless body collapsing on top of the old woman. Blood puddles formed, the air smelled of death. Like vapor or foul mist, the vehicle vanished into thin air.

"Stay here!" Hwan said, rushing out to the grisly scene.

But someone was already there, kicking the dead soldier off the old woman's shivering body and placing his coat around her shoulders.

Hoon. My hero.

Under a streetlamp in a halo of light and soft snow, Hwan and Hoon stood as true brothers. Together, they helped the old woman to her feet, walking her and the boy home, fading into darkness like kindred spirits.

The next morning, the soldiers' bodies were gone, but their blood remained on the streets as a symbol of terror that now tormented our every waking hour. There was talk among neighbors of a flight to the south where American soldiers stood post, protecting our rights and freedom from communism. But it was a dangerous passage across a border now guarded by North Korean patriot soldiers who had aligned themselves with the Red Army.

I was confused.

Who were our allies? Who were our enemies?

There were no answers.

The unspeakable act of the previous night had brought blood and death to the streets of Sinuiju, but an end to my brothers' hostile feuding. At last, their ugly battles were a thing of the past. They were fraternal twins and eternal brothers.

Now Hwan and Hoon were working together to plan our escape out of Sinuiju.

"We have to go south," Hoon told Oma. "There's nothing left for us here in this Godforsaken hell hole, except inevitable doom."

"I've heard many are already settled in Seoul," Hwan added. "The Americans are protecting our rights."

Oma agreed with a resigned nod. "We need to hire a guide. It has become too dangerous for all of you to stay in Sinuiju."

"But, Oma, you are coming with us," Hwan said.

"No, I will stay here," she said. "But Apa is already in Seoul."

"What do you mean Apa is in Seoul?" Hoon said, bewildered. "Oma, how do you know?"

"A messenger through the church sent word. Soldiers invaded the countryside, but fortunately, he escaped a few days before his secret hiding place was raided. He should be waiting for you in Seoul."

"Waiting for *us*. Oma, we are not leaving you behind," Hwan said.

"I cannot leave my orphans," she insisted. "They need me."

I was speechless, stunned, infuriated. *They* needed her? What about her own children? How could Oma stay behind? What was she thinking?

"But *we* need you too," Hoon pleaded. "Apa needs you."

"You will be fine," she said. "Apa as well."

"No, we won't be fine," I now spoke up.

"Yes, you will, Miyooki," she stated, looking away. "Your brothers will take good care of you."

Oma could hide her face, but she couldn't hide the truth. She loved her orphans more than us. Maybe I had always known it, maybe it was obvious in her day-to-day actions, but this was like no other day and hearing her decision to stay behind for the orphans broke my heart.

I asked her, "Why do you love the orphans more than us?"

"Miyooki, you know that is not true," she said, taking a step towards me.

But I backed away, shaking. "Then what is the truth, Oma? Please tell me so I can understand."

Oma was clearly disturbed by my bold behavior, but I didn't care. After all, yet again her orphans came before me.

"This is the truth, Miyooki," she said. "You were born

into good fortune. You are loved above all whether you believe it or not. You have been provided for since birth. You have never known a day of hunger."

"You are wrong, Oma. I was hungry every single day of the war effort, but you weren't here to know either way. You were too busy with your orphans."

Oma's eyes could tell a story, and right now they told the story of deep disappointment in her daughter. "I am talking about hunger that only poor children know, Miyooki. The kind of hunger that ravages the body and spirit. The kind of hunger that makes you yearn for a bowl of soy sauce water, not a bowl of warm udon noodles at your favorite restaurant. If I put my orphans before my own children, then they would be going to Seoul, not you."

Words just words that I didn't believe. Why was Oma punishing me for all the orphans and their misfortune?

"Oma, when you go to bed at night, who do you pray for first, us or your orphans?"

"Miyooki, you saw the abandoned children with your own eyes. They have nothing in this world but a few helping hands. Don't be blinded by selfishness."

Yes, I saw the orphans just as I saw Song-ho and all the children in the dye factory, and the old woman attacked outside our door. I saw dead Russian soldiers, their blood oozing from mortal wounds. No, I wasn't immune to the tragedy of our world. And while I admired Oma's devotion to those less fortunate, I would never accept her choice to sacrifice her family for her calling.

"Oma, you can't save the world, so quit trying so hard."

"My mind is made up," she firmly stated. "When the political climate settles down, you will return home and we will be together again."

Oma left the room, retreating to her quarters.

My brothers tried to console me. "It was no different when we were growing up, Miyooki," Hwan said. "Sometimes Oma and Apa were gone for weeks on missions. At least when you were born, they stayed in Sinuiju to do their work. But it's no secret. Oma and Apa are great providers, but they lack the maternal and paternal instincts."

"Not entirely true," Hoon said. "When we were babies, they strapped us to their backs and trekked all over China with other missionaries. But once we reached school-age, we were left at home with Ajumah. Poor woman."

"Miyooki," Hwan said. "Another fact, Oma's faith comes before everything. Ask any of her relatives. They will tell you that she is the female vision of Jesus."

"And we are just one small family in her global view of life, little one," Hoon said, his voice tinged with resentment. "Why do you think she gave Dai money that we needed?"

"I just want her to come with us," I said. "I'm sure there are plenty of orphans in Seoul who need her help."

"Let it go, Miyooki," Hwan said.

No, I wouldn't let Oma stay behind without a fight. Frustrated, I turned my back on Hwan and Hoon, and I marched into my parents' quarters to confront Oma. I found her in the walk-in closet, on her knees at the safe, retrieving the burlap sack Apa had given her before we'd boarded the train from Sogha to Sinuiju. She looked so small, childlike. I suddenly grew sad, stifling my tears. She opened the sack, revealing a cache of valuables: jewels, silk, gold coins… but what caught my eye was a triangular wooden case with a silver clasp deep inside the safe.

"Oma, what's that?" I asked her.

Oma proceeded to slowly open the wooden case, her small, delicate hands unfolding layers of white material tucked inside. She raised what appeared to be a banner with a red and blue circle in the middle and black symbols in each corner, some broken, some not.

"The Korean flag," she whispered as though the mere words were taboo.

"I never knew we had our own flag," I murmured.

"There are many things you don't know or understand right now, Miyooki. You need time to live, grow, and learn."

"But, Oma, how can I grow when you hide things from me? I should have known about *our* flag."

"For many years, it was illegal to own a Korean flag. This flag belonged to your haraboji. It is sacred to our family. Apa and I didn't show you the flag to protect you, just as I am now by sending you to Seoul."

As Oma explained to me, Korea's elusive flag had been banished from our country decades earlier. It was replaced by the Japanese flag—the one raised at the Ichiban School with a giant red circle against a white banner background, better known as *Hinomaru* or the circle of the sun.

"Our flag is beautiful," I said. "What do the symbols mean?"

"The white background represents peace and purity," Oma said. "The circle represents the cosmic forces of light and dark, hot and cold, which give our world perfect balance, much like the Chinese belief of yin and yang."

"Or Hwan and Hoon," I suggested.

Oma smiled. "Yes, like your brothers."

"What about the black symbols in each corner?"

Oma pointed to the top left and bottom right symbols. "Heaven and earth." She then pointed to the top right and left bottom symbols. "Fire and water. Each symbol is positioned to its opposing nature."

Night and day. Heaven and earth. Good and evil. Love and hate. Rich and poor. I had no choice but to accept Oma's decision to remain in Sinuiju with her orphans. I was devastated, but I couldn't fight the cosmic forces of nature and that of humans.

8

GOODBYE, OMA

*Oma hugged me, her breath shallow, her heart beating
like a dying dove...*

Oma carefully folded the Korean flag, placing it back into
the wooden case and sealing the silver clasp. She slid the case
deep into a dark pocket of the safe, hiding the symbol of
peace and harmony with random objects—a bamboo-framed
photo of Apa, a satin-beaded purse, a pair of baby *comoshin*
slippers. Turning her attention to the burlap sack, she mulled
over its contents with a shrewd eye, touching jewels with her
own pearl-like fingertips, caressing silk, counting gold coins.

"All of this belonged to your halmoni," she spoke. "They
were part of her wedding dowry. Passed down to me, now
they belong to you in the care of your brothers. You will
take the dowry with you on your journey to the South, only
relinquishing these riches to spare your life."

Yes, I was overwhelmed by fear, but more so, I was overcome by deep love and sadness.

"Oma—" I wept.

"Please, Miyooki, no tears," she said, her voice cracking.
"You must be brave for me, braver than you have ever been
before. Do you understand?"

"Yes, Oma."

February was cold and quiet, as silent as Sogha at midnight.
Above us the stars were so big you could almost touch them
or fool yourself into believing so. In the city, we endured a
dreamless kind of silence without hope, without stars. At

night, even the Red Army sought warmth from the Siberian-like temperatures. And while I missed Apa dearly, I ran a gamut of emotions from anger to feelings of abandonment. The swiftness of his departure had left me little time to absorb the consequences. To leave us was to protect us, that's what he had said. But now I wondered. After all, no one was safe in our city anymore. Pillaging, assault, murder had been going on for months now. How could Apa not have known what was coming? How could he escape to Seoul, leaving us trapped in the crossfire of Red Army bullets aimed at a group of young men who called themselves the New Resistance?

"Who exactly are these men?" I asked Hoon.

"Foolish teenage boys."

"But why foolish? They're the voice of freedom."

"This is not an organized faction of resistance, little one. They are only provoking violence."

"With peaceful marches?"

"Believe me, they will end up in jail or worse, dead."

Hoon was right.

One morning I awoke to the foot-stomping chants of resistance. "Leave our country! Leave our country!" and "Commies, go home! Commies, go home!"

Their words were empowering, if for a moment. For what followed was a round of bullets so loud and murderous, I covered my ears. In a violent flash, voices were hushed, freedom crushed. The only sound was the death song delivered by witnesses to the carnage. Twenty-four teenaged boys died that day, their river of blood dashing any hope for peace.

Was Apa aware of the slaughter on the streets of Sinuiju? Was he frantically awaiting our arrival, torturing himself over our fate in what Hoon called a godforsaken hell hole? Or had he settled into a new life in Seoul without a thought as to what was going on up north? Did he even know Oma was staying behind with her orphans?

"I feel like Apa has forgotten us," I told Hoon one evening

as we sat outside on the daecheong, staring at the night sky, watching our breath smoke then vanish among the stars.

Hoon cracked his cocky smile, the one that revealed a small gap between his front teeth, a gap Oma claimed was a sign of good fortune. Hwan's long earlobes, too, were a sign that his luck would never run out. I hoped Oma was right.

"Yes, little one," Hoon teased me. "I imagine our righteous Apa left us for a new life in the south. He probably has a new young bride and a child on the way."

"Stop making fun of me," I said.

"But you're a funny girl," he insisted.

Now I smiled. Hoon could always bring a little joy to an otherwise gloomy world. Even now, as war loomed over our country, he could lull me into a false sense of security with his humor.

"But I don't understand why I ever came back to Sinuiju in the first place. Why didn't we all hide out with Apa in the countryside? Had we stayed together, all of us would be in Seoul right now, including Oma. Am I right?"

"Oma wasn't going anywhere," Hoon flatly stated. "And back then, no one could fathom the outcome. Only church ministers were in danger, and we were hoping that was temporary."

"But, Hoon, you yourself said it over the Chuseok holiday."

"I said what?"

"You predicted a civil war, remember?"

Hoon shrugged, his eyes lost in the stars. "Call me a prophet, little one."

Once again, Sinuiju was hit with a winter storm. Trees glistening with ice resembled glass figurines, creating a perfect snow globe world.

If only...

Business was brisk with a constant stream of midnight

callers in need of warmth that only The Hundred Choices Department Store inventory could provide at a fair price. Now the money drawer was replenished with a stack of currency that helped keep the household afloat.

One late evening, a cloaked stranger appeared at the door, someone other than a Korean acquaintance arriving to purchase a coat or gloves. Older than my brothers but younger than Apa, he stood in our parlor looking out of place like a monk who should be in a monastery. He had come to discuss plans for our journey to Seoul. Hoon told me that the man was to be our guide and was paid handsomely to map out safe routes across the border.

"Korean allies of the Red Army are now lining up on the border to 'protect' us from the Americans," Hoon said. "Anyone going south relies on a guide to help them safely cross over."

Cross over. A double meaning, one of freedom, or one of death, depending on which route one took.

"There were once many pockets along the border to easily escape," the guide said. "But now that Korean patriots are joining forces with the Red Army, all those pockets are filling up rapidly with ruthless armed soldiers. Many deaths have been reported."

Oma sat quietly, hands folded into a tight knot, just as when she prayed before meals. She looked worried, headachy, as though the weight of the world rested on her small shoulders.

"We paid you to map out safe routes," Hoon said. "Do you have them or not?"

The guide lit a cigarette, the match flame emphasizing the leathery lines of his face and hands. It occurred to me that this so-called guide could be a farmer or laborer, someone who worked the land and well knew its dips and curves and passes.

"Who said anything about 'safe' routes?" he asked. "I was

paid to survey the border and give you alternate routes into the south. If you think money can buy safety, then you are living in dreams. There is no such thing anymore."

Hwan looked out the window, his eyes glazing over. He had begun drinking heavily since the loss of The Hundred Choices Department Store. At times, he seemed a disheveled stranger. I often heard him late at night in his quarters humming old Japanese songs, and I wondered if he would ever embrace his true self. It was sad, though, to watch a once confident young man with princely airs now walk with his shoulders hunched and his head down.

"There was a time when everything he touched turned to gold," Hoon told me. "Now he's feeling lost in a world that no longer idolizes him. Even his old Jap buddy has left him for the Motherland."

A world without magic and dreams. How could Oma bear to look at Hwan, her once triumphant son who had dashed in and out of our lives with fanfare and style? Did it break her heart to see him this way?

"She compartmentalizes her pain and disappointment," Hoon told me. "How else do you think she managed to put up with me all these years?"

"What do you have for us?" Oma asked the guide.

The guide, a cigarette between his lips, removed a map from within his robe and spread it across the floor. We followed his index finger as he traced a barely visible path.

"All the details are on this map," he said. "In summary, you will take a train to Pyongyang, then a van to the countryside. There, a six-mile mountain hike awaits you before crossing a river. Be forewarned, the enemy is everywhere—on the train, on the mountain, at the border. This is your best chance for freedom, but the longer you wait, the more dangerous it will become."

"How can you expect us to go in this treacherous weather?" Hoon asked, angered. "We will die on the mountain."

"Plan your escape now," the guide said. "And when the snows melt, be prepared to leave before it is too late."

◈

Shortly after the guide left, Oma anxiously gathered staples for our journey—rice crackers, dried fish strips, almond cookies—muttering a prayer as she tossed them into a knapsack.

We looked on with tragic amusement.

Hwan sobered up, realizing the gravity of the situation. "Oma, please, we aren't going anywhere tonight."

"You heard the guide," she said. "Be prepared to leave at a moment's notice."

Later that evening, Oma told me to pack essentials and nothing else for my trip.

"A change of clothes, an extra pair of shoes, and a blanket," she said. "Everything else can be purchased once you are in Seoul."

Everything, but my Chuseok moon, which I carefully placed inside my knapsack.

"And your silk pouch," Ajumah reminded me.

Of course, how could I forget my beloved silk pouch filled with shiny pebbles, the only remnants I had left of Sogha? What would I do without Ajumah, my right arm, my friend, my confidant? In my heart, I knew she wasn't coming with us to Seoul, for her life was here, however tragic. But I asked her anyway.

"Ajumah, are you going to Seoul with us?"

"I will stay here," she said. "Like the orphans need your oma, your oma needs me."

Yes, Oma needed Ajumah, we all needed her. But the truth was, she was staying behind, hopeful that her grandson—her only link to a family besides ours that I was aware of—would one day show up at the doorstep. Ajumah was the rock of our family, the unassuming worker who rarely spoke of her own offspring. At the same time, she took care of all of us, and yet we failed to ease her quiet grief.

"Ajumah?"

"Yes, Miyooki."

"Is it true that your husband was murdered by the Japanese police?"

"Yes, but there were circumstances."

"What kind of circumstances?"

"The Japanese had recently taken over the country. My husband and I were a young married couple, out having a good time at the local teahouse. The teahouse offered rice wine to the male patrons. Of course, my husband could not resist, and ended up drinking too much. Well"—she giggled like a blushing new bride—"too much for him was actually very little. It was late when we left the teahouse, and he was singing, laughing, and stumbling the whole way home when two Japanese policemen stopped us. Instead of answering their questions like he had always done when we were interrogated on the streets, he reacted the way I imagine Hoon would."

"Oh no," I moaned.

Ajumah sighed. "Yes, quite combatively. He actually took a swing at one of the policemen, and that is when they—"

"Killed him?"

Ajumah sighed again, growing emotional. "Right before my very eyes. They threw him to the ground and kicked him over and over until he was dead. I begged for his life, but it was useless. Why couldn't he just answer their questions? All the years we lost over too much rice wine."

"Oh, Ajumah," I cried. "I'm so sorry!"

"A few weeks later, I found out I was pregnant with our daughter."

"You raised your daughter alone?"

"In a sense, yes, but I went to live at home with my parents where my daughter grew up like a princess in a way I never did. But nothing can replace a father's love."

"Where is your daughter now?"

"She and her husband are missionaries in China. They haven't seen their son for a year now, but like Oma, their faith keeps them going."

"You must miss them."

"Very much."

While I was sad to say goodbye to Ajumah, I took comfort in knowing she would be here for Oma as she had been for me on Sogha mountain.

"I will miss you," I said.

"I will miss you too, Miyooki. We must take this time to emotionally prepare for your departure. It will be a very difficult day for all of us."

Winter's harsh snowstorms had shielded us from the evils of mankind and protected us from random acts of violence. Now that it was spring, flashes of forsythia brightened the city landscape, but the Red Army emerged from their long hibernation, roaming the streets in search of trouble. Many armed Korean soldiers and police officers aligned themselves with the Russians to form a communist regime. Who were these Korean men, I wondered, before they morphed into monsters with machine guns?

"They were lost boys who played stick ball in the street with me," Hoon told me. "Thanks to the Japs, they grew up to be angry Korean men who hate outsiders. That could have been me out there, little one. But I had Oma and Apa who never gave up on their troubled son, who guided me away from the streets."

We all knew Hoon was the rebellious son who resented the Japanese, but he wasn't a "true Korean patriot," someone with hate in his eyes who hungered for power and notoriety, a cold-blooded murderer.

❧

Oma looked out the window, clutching a porcelain teacup,

her index finger outlining a painted pink flower. Steam rose from the cup like a smokescreen, but it couldn't hide her far-away gaze, the distance between where she stood and where her thoughts had taken her. In the courtyard, the delicate cherry blossoms were in full bloom, their fleeting beauty a reminder that everything came to an end.

"You will leave tonight," Oma murmured.

For the last couple of months, I had done as Ajumah advised me. I had prepared mentally for this moment, tell-ing myself over and over that I was ready to journey south with my brothers. But nothing could have prepared me for this farewell. Nothing. Parting ways with Apa had been hard enough. A temporary separation, that's what he'd told me, until order was restored. I had believed him and understood his departure to be an emergency action, one no different than a typhoon evacuation that would lift when the storm moved out to sea. But this storm stalled and hovered over Sinuiju like a black cloud of death.

Now I was to lose Oma too.

"Stay with your brothers at all times," Oma said. "Do not speak to anyone on the train as there will be spies looking for people who are fleeing. If you are questioned, you are visiting your aunt and uncle in Pyongyang. Explain that they will be waiting for you at the train station."

I was confused. "But, Oma, we have never visited an aunt and uncle in Pyongyang."

"Miyooki, listen carefully," Oma said. "The two people you are meeting at the train station in Pyongyang are not your aunt and uncle, but that is the story you will tell if you are questioned on the train. Do you understand?"

"Yes, Oma."

"The man and woman you are meeting in Pyongyang are actually hired guides who cross the border for business deal-ings and are well-acquainted with policemen and soldiers. With them by your side, you will not be interrogated. The woman will be carrying a black purse with a large gold clasp, and the man will be wearing a gray hat tipped to one side. He is the same man who came to our house last winter."

"The monk?"

Oma nodded. "Yes, Miyooki, but he is not a monk, but a man who wears many hats, literally and figuratively. He has posed as a doctor, a businessman, an artist, and, yes, even a monk. He and the woman will take you to the foot of the mountain and give you an updated map to follow to the river. From there, you and your brothers will be on your own. Once you reach the river, the lights to freedom will guide you across the border."

"Lights to freedom?"

"South Korean freedom patriots stand post on the other side of the river, flashing lights, guiding freedom seekers to safety."

The evening air was chilly but fragrant with lilacs, lilies, and sweet honeysuckle. Memories of better times came rushing back to me with the emotional force of monsoon-swollen river waters—spring days, before World War II changed everything, when I was too young and naïve to know that nothing was as it seemed. Afternoons in the shopping district, enjoying plum tea and rice cakes with Hoon. I closed my eyes, not wanting this moment to pass, not wanting to say goodbye. But then we were at the gate, ready to depart. I looked back at the house, barely visible in the blue dusk, striving to memorize every inch of stone, wood, and tile, wondering how long I would be away from my beloved home.

I turned to Ajumah first. "Goodbye, dear friend," I said. She hugged me hard. "I will write you letters."

I didn't want to let her go.

But, alas, then it was Oma's turn. She held me close. "Who are you visiting in Pyongyang?" she quizzed me.

"We are visiting our aunt and uncle," I said, tears streaming down my cheeks.

"Good girl," she whispered, slipping lemon candies in my pocket.

"Oma…" I wept.

"Shh…" she hushed me, holding me tight, her breath shallow, her heart beating like a dying dove.

9

JOURNEY SOUTH

He was dressed in civilian clothing and paced up and down the aisle, scrutinizing each passenger with a penetrating eye...

As if time had stopped that spring night in 1946, a part of me would always be a fifteen-year-old girl standing at the gate with Oma and Ajumah, saying our gut-wrenching goodbyes. And, yet, walking beyond the wall of our compound was a liberating moment, my first step towards freedom.

To my surprise, Sinuiju was relatively busy with folks milling about town, enjoying the mild weather and makeshift open markets that sold fruits and vegetables, fresh fish, and whole chickens. A few bakeries and restaurants were open, but most were filled with groups of Korean police and Red Army officers. Civilians had little money for such luxuries or the desire to share space with the enemy; instead, they opted for moonlit strolls down the street. Koreans were tired of being cooped up inside their compounds, tired of moving cautiously through the streets to avoid confrontation with soldiers and police, tired of living in constant fear. Oma had told me to be brave, and the spirit of the people made me feel so.

I was ready to journey in the dark, over a mountain and across a river in the quest for freedom.

We followed a familiar path to the train station, the same path I had taken for many years on my way to school. Construction was underway along the shopping district, with demolished buildings reduced to piles of rubble. What buildings might replace my old haunts and The Hundred Choices

Department Store didn't pique my curiosity one bit. I looked away, keeping my memories of the past alive.

Before boarding the train, Hwan turned his head and took a quick swig of rice wine, then tucked the small flask in his jacket, hoping no one took note. My heart broke for my stumbling brother. Apa once called Hoon the lost brother. He was wrong. If we survived our journey south, I wondered what would become of Hwan. Would he ever find his footing again? Would he ever walk tall as he used to do?

I took my seat between my brothers, looking out the window and clutching my silk pouch, trying to avoid eye contact with other passengers, suspicious that anyone could be a spy, even the young boy sitting in front of me. The smell of fear was in the air, and I sensed there were many others with the same plan: To escape the tyranny of what was now an established government, formed to strip citizens of their freedom, to reduce us to human puppets and slaves.

"The Provisional People's Committee," Hwan had said the night before, drinking rice wine as if it were water. "Spearheaded by a Korean man trained by the Soviets who hated the Japanese. Rumor has it that he was a major in the Red Army."

"He is nothing but a worthless communist guerrilla," Hoon added. "A Russian patsy! Exiled so long ago, he barely speaks Korean!"

I didn't fully understand all that my brothers were saying, but I knew this new leader was the cause of our troubles.

The train ride to Pyongyang took less than two hours, but it felt like a slow death as I spotted a man who was, I was certain, one of the spies Oma had warned us about. He was dressed in civilian clothing and paced up and down the aisle, scrutinizing each passenger with a penetrating eye. I was learning that where there was man, there was evil. I clutched my silk pouch, gazing fixedly out the window, following the spy's reflection in the glass, hoping to blend in.

But it was impossible to keep a low profile in the company of my brothers. Even dressed down in black slacks and the most modest of jackets offered at The Hundred Choices Department Store, Hwan and Hoon stood out in any crowd. With their good looks and tall stature, they were the envy of all men, and this small, ugly Korean man was no exception. He paused in front of us, observing my brothers with that familiar begrudging eye I had seen many times before. Hwan and Hoon held his stare. The spy, they knew, likely had a concealed weapon. Still, he was intimidated by my brothers, and like all bullies, targeted a lesser person, someone smaller and timid.

He picked on me.

"You, looking out the window," he said. "What is in your pouch?"

At this point, Hoon would normally come to my defense and take the bully down. But this man before us was a government spy who had been granted permission to kill, and if provoked, would likely do just that.

I opened my pouch, took out the colorful pebbles, and held them in my hand for the spy to inspect. He squinted at them with curious wonder. After all, they were beautiful. For a moment, I actually saw a human behind those cold, cruel eyes.

"From Sogha mountain," I said. "Would you like one?"

I raised my palm towards the spy, offering him a pebble of his choice, holding my breath.

A small but sincere smile crossed the spy's face, as if acknowledging human kindness was an act of treason.

"Enjoy your ride," he said before walking away.

I slowly exhaled.

The train finally pulled into Pyongyang. Just as Oma had promised, two guides—a woman holding a black purse with a large gold clasp, and the monk, now looking dapper in a gray fedora hat slightly tipped to one side—were waiting for us. On cue, we embraced our so-called aunt and uncle like family, performing our parts as if on stage under spotlights. In truth, with all the armed policemen roaming the train station, we were playing the most important role of our lives.

Arm-in-arm with our "aunt and uncle," we slipped away from the station hub and down a dark, quiet street to a waiting van. The man gave Hoon a map, and before we could say thank you or goodbye, the duo disappeared, vanishing like a magic act.

The van was already crowded with men, women, and children who had also been on the train. We sat on the floor of the van in silence, keeping to ourselves. No one spoke or let their eyes meet for fear there might still be a spy among us.

Part one of our journey had now been successfully completed.

As the van started its engine, I rested my head on Hoon's shoulder, closing my eyes. The ride was cramped and bumpy, and the unpleasant smell of human sweat made me queasy.

"I feel sick to my stomach," I whispered to Hoon.

"Eat one of your candies," he reminded me.

Yes, my lemon candies! I was quickly learning that Oma was always looking after me, at home and from afar. I dug into my pocket for a candy and popped it into my mouth, the sweet tartness quelling my nausea, making the ride bearable. Again, I thought about Song-ho and wondered where he was, what he was doing. I hoped he had found good people who had changed his life for the better.

Two hours later we arrived at our destination—the middle of nowhere. The crowd clambered out of the van, scattering like mice on separate journeys, all with one destination: freedom. But a dark and ghostly mountain chain stood between us, one more haunting than the night sky. Unlike Sogha's sunny paths, lined with birds and butterflies, this route was rugged and dangerous, with precipitous drops and slippery rocks. I turned to my brothers. Their tension was infectious—Hwan swigging from his flask, Hoon holding my hand too tightly—but together they were my compass in the dark, navigating me up the steep mountain. Hoon led the way. Hwan was the anchor. I kept turning around, making sure he was still behind me.

"Stop looking back, Miyooki," he said. "Don't worry, I'm here."

But my heartstrings were already tugging me back, far beyond Hwan and the mountain, to Sinuiju, to happier times, to peaceful times before our world went up in smoke. Haunting memories slowed me down—of trying on lavish jewelry at The Hundred Choices Department Store after hours, counting the stars above Sogha mountain, school days before the war effort made it a living hell, ice-skating on the Amrok River at twilight, Apa's sermons and Oma's prayers that always summoned deep emotion, Ajumah's steady presence, Hwan's sanguine smile, Hoon's mockery of life...

Just when I thought my memories could shield me from this cold black mountain, thunderous gunfire shattered my hopes. Birds flocked to the sky in alarm, and my hand slipped from Hoon's as we fell to the ground, paralyzed, holding our breath as another round of bullets passed through the trees. Then there was silence, an eerie kind of silence that spoke of blood and death. It was also our cue to run for our lives. I ran fast, faster, until my legs cramped and my lungs burned fire, until I slipped and tumbled to the ground. Hwan helped me to my feet. My knees oozed blood, but I pushed forward, not wanting to die on the mountain. Still, I couldn't keep up with Hoon who moved with lightning strides.

"Slow down!" Hwan whisper-shouted.

"There is no slowing down," Hoon whisper-shouted back. "We have to make it to the river before dawn! It's our only chance to sneak by border patrols!"

And so, I trudged on, never once complaining, silent tears

of pain running down my cheeks. Even when I stumbled and fell to my raw and bloodied knees, I said nothing. But at that point, I thought, Hoon was welcome to leave me on the mountain at the mercy of wild animals in his quest for freedom. I couldn't go any further.

"Stop, Hoon!" Hwan cried this time. He didn't give a damn who heard him, and neither did I.

Hoon paused before turning around. I could read his mind. He was torn, knowing a few minutes could mean the difference between freedom gained and freedom lost, between life and death. But he made his choice and came running back to us.

"Fifteen minutes," he said. "That's all we can spare. Miyooki, you have to summon the natural athlete in you for our final push across the border."

Maybe I didn't want freedom as much as Hoon. Instead, I envisioned a patrol ambush forcing us back to a mythical Sinuiju where The Hundred Choices Department Store's neon sign still lit up the gateway to our beloved city. But the distant sound of gunfire brought me back to our doomed world.

Hwan spread out a blanket for us to sit on. The fresh mountain air was sobering him, I thought, or perhaps his flask was finally empty of rice wine. Either way, I was happy. Hoon gave us each two honey cookies that Ajumah and I had made the day before. How I longed for the last Chuseok. How I longed to be back on Sogha mountain, rolling dough with Ajumah. I could still smell the heavenly cookies frying in oil. I could still see Oma's eyes brighten as she took her first bite.

Hoon took out a small map tucked inside his sock. Under the light of the moon, he carefully read our route. "It's approximately four miles to the river," he said. "What time is it?"

To my surprise, Hwan pulled out a plain pocket watch that

had belonged to Apa. The understated style of this time-piece suited Apa well, but not Hwan. Times had changed. Where was Hwan's flashy Rolex Oyster wristwatch with eighteen-karat gold that told far more than just the time? Hoon would likely claim that Dai Takagi had stolen Hwan's watch right off his wrist, but having seen the bedecked arms of Russian soldiers, I wasn't so sure.

"Just past midnight," Hwan said.

"We're averaging a little over a mile an hour," Hoon calculated. "We need to get moving again."

My tired legs weren't ready to go anywhere just yet. And besides, I wanted the taste of honey to linger on my lips. Was that too much to ask?

"Please, Hoon," I begged him, no longer a brave girl.

But my plea fell on deaf ears as moments later we were back on the rocky trail, moving slowly and cautiously along the jagged edge. The night air was cold on my cheeks, and the howls of wild animals sounded all around us. Hoon moved quickly, racing against daylight, and I struggled to keep up.

"Faster, Miyooki!" Hwan urged. "Just like Oma said, once we see the lights, we'll be close to freedom."

Hours later, we finally descended the mountain and a miracle happened. I looked up and saw a beacon of hope—the heavenly glow of lights tempting me across the river. My energy surged, and my pace quickened. Once I heard the rushing waters, I moved with buoyant footsteps, knowing our journey was almost over. I could smell the earthy river and taste freedom. But a sudden flash of light, sweeping through the woods in every direction, paralyzed us in our tracks. Then came the sound of barking dogs, followed by shrieking, an explosion of gunshots, then gruesome silence. We held our breath, statue still, for what seemed a lifetime. Was it safe to move on? It was too quiet, eerily so, as if border patrols and their menacing dogs were about to pounce on us from every direction.

"We have to cross the river now!" Hoon said. "It's our only chance. Daylight is less than an hour away."

"Let me go first," Hwan suggested.

"No!" I cried. "We cross together or not at all, that's what Oma said. She told me to stay with both of you at all times. And if we're stopped by patrols to offer them my dowry to spare our lives."

Hwan was steadfast. "Miyooki, Oma isn't here to tell us what to do. If we stay together, we're as good as dead."

Hoon agreed. "Once Hwan is halfway across the river, you will follow."

The three of us huddled, forming a sibling bond. But just as in life, Hwan broke away too soon, ready for his final task.

"No!" I cried, again, pulling him back to the circle. "We have to go together!"

Hoon, frustrated, knowing there was no time for arguments, glanced up and down the river, brainstorming. "Okay, little one, have it your way," he said. "We'll cross at the same time, but from different points of the river. Hwan will go twenty-five meters east and I will go twenty-five meters west. At the count of sixty, we enter the river. Is that clear?"

"Yes," Hwan said.

"Yes," I said too.

Just the thought of splitting up frightened me. But fear aside, Hoon's plan made the most sense. Before parting ways, he placed the contents of Oma's dowry in my knapsack. Then we held each other tightly one last time.

"See you both on the other side," Hoon said.

My brothers left me, heading in opposite directions, starting their count. "One, two, three…"

Four, five, six, seven… I continued, counting in my head until I got to sixty.

Like a turtle hatchling making its way towards the safety of water, I quickly crawled along the riverbank, trying to escape a hidden predator. Finally, reaching my destination,

I dipped my head below the cold, shallow water and swam, goosebumps covering my body, relief washing over me. Just when I thought freedom was a few strokes away, a stitch of bullets hit the water, causing a rippling effect. When I came up for air, I heard a voice shout from the north bank.

"Out of the water!"

More gunshots exploded in the sky above my head. I looked around for Hwan and Hoon, but there was no sign of my brothers anywhere. Had they made it to the freedom land? I prayed so. Like a white flag, I raised both hands in the air and turned back, trudging out of the water, my hope for freedom dashed.

"On your knees!" one of two border patrolmen ordered.

I dropped to my knees like a ragdoll, almost too exhausted to be afraid. Almost. One of the patrolmen grabbed my hair, yanking my head backward, and pressed the cold, steely barrel of his gun firmly against my temple. The other patrolman shone his light on my face, blinding me.

"Why are you trying to cross the river?" he demanded, knowing perfectly well my reasons.

No matter what I said, I knew the outcome would remain the same. Like those many other victims on the mountain side, I was going to die an anonymous death, but not until this ugly man's slow and torturous interrogation was over. Still, I wouldn't answer him, and I would not die with my eyes closed. I heard Ajumah's voice in my head: *Look to the stars, Miyooki.* I did just that. Perhaps hope had run out for me, but my eyes were trained on those magnificent stars. And no matter how upset Oma would be with me, I refused to offer up my dowry in exchange for my life. These men would, I knew, take all the precious jewels, then shoot me anyway.

"Answer the question, traitor!" the man insisted, his gun pressed to my head.

But I said nothing, keeping my eyes on the stars as thoughts whirled through my mind—I thought of my family, whom I would never see again, the mark that I would never make in the world, all my memories soon to be obliterated with one explosive gunshot. But I also thought about this: I was forever part of a greater action, seeking freedom from the evil clutches of tyranny.

The patrolman pulled back the trigger of his gun, preparing to fire, and I took my last breath, never wavering, accepting my fate…when lo and behold came my saving grace.

"Let her go," the other patrolman said.

"Are you crazy?" he replied, keeping his gun firmly to my temple. "Her head is worth a sack of rice, half for me, half for you!"

"The next sack of rice belongs to you," the other said. "All of it. Now let her go."

"Why is this one so special?" the patrolman asked. "Do you know her?"

"Yes," the other said, lowering his flashlight, and as he did so, I recognized the boy in rags who had been hunched over the dye vats; a boy with sweet, sad eyes; a boy who had once loved lemon candies. Even in the predawn light I recognized him. His eyes had hardened, and he was taller now, dressed in fatigues and holding a machine gun, but it was still Song-ho.

"She once did me a favor," Song-ho continued. "Now I must return the favor."

I heard Oma's words: *Small gestures are never forgotten.*

Song-ho's partner grunted. Removing the gun barrel from my head, he shoved me to the ground and walked away, his mind already on the hunt for his next head, knowing a full bag of rice belonged to him.

"Go!" Song-ho urged me. "Before my compatriot changes his mind!"

I wanted to beg Song-ho to come with me, to tell him that I had plenty of lemon candies in my pocket to share. But it was too late. The once timid factory boy now had blood on his hands. He now stood tall, empowered by the new regime. So I ran to the river and swam for my life, never looking back, moving towards those heavenly lights flashing on the other side. *Goodbye, Sinuiju! Goodbye, Ajumah! Goodbye, Oma!* Halfway across the river, I heard the cheering voices of freedom patriots exclaim: "Welcome to the freedom land!"

10

FREEDOM

*Song-ho spared my life, true, but the orphan had
morphed into a monster...*

Before I took my first breath of freedom, American soldiers
sprayed me with chemicals, just as farmers dusted the rice
fields to vanquish mosquitoes. I held my breath, shielding
my face.

After the soldiers were done with me, two peace-loving
strangers—a young man and woman—came to my rescue,
wrapping my body in blankets and serving me tea and bis-
cuits.

"We are freedom patriots," they told me. "Welcome to the
freedom land!"

I was shivering violently from both the cold river and
trauma I had endured, but I was grateful to have new friends
in the south. "Why did they spray me?" I asked, humiliated.

"All refugees are sprayed with DDT before boarding the
train to prevent the spread of disease," the man said, apolo-
getically.

"But now is the time to celebrate!" the woman exclaimed.
"You are free!"

"Have you seen my brothers?" I asked them. "Two tall
men in their twenties wearing all black, named Hwan and
Hoon."

As my new friends mulled over my descriptions, I suddenly heard Hoon's voice above the bell of freedom that always
rang whenever another refugee came to shore.

"Miyooki!"

"Hoon!" I called out, frantically searching for my brother in the crowd. Then his glorious face appeared in the dawning light. "Over here!"

Hoon and I embraced, euphoric to be together again.

"Thank God, you're alive," he murmured.

"They almost killed me, Hoon. But they let me go…because of…of lemon candies!" I stammered, overcome by a renewed hysteria following my brush with death.

"Shh," Hoon said, rocking me in his arms. "It's over, little one. You don't have to think about *them* anymore. We are free."

Yes, we were free, and my near-death experience was now behind me, left on the wrong side of the border, where desperate young boys had been brainwashed to become killers. Here in the south, we thanked our new friends for their love and support.

"Godspeed to you both!" they chorused, before moving on to the next wave of refugees.

I turned back to Hoon. "Have you seen Hwan?"

My brother's face suddenly darkened, his lips trembling with grief.

"No…" I murmured in disbelief, cursing the god who had just saved my life, cursing myself for never loving Hwan as much as I loved Hoon. And now he was dead, gone forever.

"No!" I wailed, burying my face in Hoon's chest.

"Miyooki! Miyooki! Hwan is alive!" he assured me. "But he is injured, shot in the leg by a border patrol."

Was it Song-ho who had shot Hwan? How many of his victims were maimed or dead on the mountain or in the river? How many sacks of rice had he collected that morning? Song-ho had spared my life, true, but the orphan had morphed into a monster.

"Where is Hwan now?"

"With Apa on his way to the hospital in Seoul."

I couldn't believe my ears. "Apa is here?"

Hoon nodded. "He helped Freedom Patriots pull Hwan out of the water! The train station isn't far. If we leave now, we can catch the next train directly to the hospital."

I almost died. Hwan was shot. Apa was waiting for us... The world was spinning, my head reeling with emotion.

We arrived at the hospital just as the sun made its way over the mountaintop.

We asked for Hwan, but our query was drowned out by emergency room chaos—the rush of paramedics through the double doors, the cries of patients, and others, like us, worried for their loved ones.

But soon we found Apa clutching his Bible, praying as he slowly limped across the floor, leaning heavily on a cane. Gone was the man with the strength of Samson. Apa's gray-flecked hair was now pure white, his posture hunched, and a deep scar marred his forehead. The sight of him made me sob with joy and grief. As he held me in his arms, I was gripped with guilt. I wanted God to punish me, to strike me down for all my faithlessness. Of course, Apa loved us! Of course, he had worried day and night, suffering through fitful sleep, feeling helpless from afar—all this while struggling with his own ailments. Like the stars and the moon—and like Oma—Apa was always there.

"Hoon, Miyooki," he breathed, his voice as unsteady as his gait.

"Apa," I wept.

"What happened to you?" Hoon asked.

"It's a very long story," Apa replied. "But let us focus all our thoughts on Hwan. He is in surgery. The bullet shattered his femur but missed a major artery. Now we wait."

As we sat, watching the clock, I told Apa and Hoon all about my own brush with death and how the factory boy had spared my life. "The other patrolman wanted to kill me for a sack of rice, but Song-ho saved me. Oma once said, 'small gestures are never forgotten.' She was right."

Hoon choked up. "It was karma, little one."

"A miracle," Apa breathed. "Or perhaps an act of God. Either way, I am forever thankful to Song-ho."

I was thankful too, but Hwan was in surgery. Maybe it wasn't Song-ho's bullet that had shattered my brother's leg, but the factory boy was one of *them* now, the enemy.

"This is for you," Hoon said to Apa, retrieving a wet envelope from his soaked knapsack.

Apa opened the envelope and proceeded to read the handwritten letter penned by Oma. I would never know its contents, but judging by Apa's heartbroken expression, he was a man who had just lost his beloved wife.

"Did you know Oma intended to stay in Sinuiju with her orphans?" I asked.

"Yes," Apa replied. "We must pray that our country chooses a peaceful solution over war. Then we can all go home."

Hoon was doubtful. "Sinuiju is already a war zone, Apa. The people are brainwashed by propaganda and fear. Song-ho is not the only poor boy they are recruiting."

I agreed. "Song-ho was once an innocent orphan, but now he is a murderer. If only Oma had found him first. Maybe then he would be at the church instead of at the border killing innocent people!"

"Miyooki, Hoon, please, try not to judge," Apa said. "You must understand—"

"Understand what, Apa?" I demanded. "That it's okay for poor children to grow up to be evil?"

"No, you must understand that Korea has been under siege throughout time. We are a land of riches that outsiders hunger for. And our country is strategically located, hence Japan's rule for many decades. A new leader has risen in the north, a man who promises self-rule. Impoverished young men have been promised a better life. You can't blame them for having hope, no matter how empty this new leader's promises might be. Hunger, after all, breeds desperation."

"But you heard Hoon, Apa! It's all propaganda. And war is going to break out."

"Only time will tell, Miyooki."

"War or no war, I hate the Russians!" I cried. "I hate the North Koreans! They are all evil monsters!"

"Miyooki," Apa hushed me. "Please, do not hate."

"She has been through hell, Apa," Hoon said. "You can't blame her for feeling this way. Like the Japs, the Commies have destroyed many families."

"And Russian soldiers helped me cross the border," Apa countered. "Have a seat, and I will tell you a story."

Apa shared his story of a harrowing journey south, all alone. It had been early winter when he left the countryside. The frozen mountain was covered with ice. Even on sunny days, the ice remained thick and treacherous, for the temperature never rose above twenty degrees.

"I moved slowly but slipped anyway, tumbling down the mountainside," he told us.

Apa had sustained deep cuts to his head and face, and worse, he'd broken his left hip. Cold and exposed for a day and a night, countless guides and Korean refugees walked past him.

"They all left me to die," Apa sighed, feeling the kind of disappointment only a man of the cloth can feel, one who has always sustained a deep and abiding faith in mankind. "It was easier to just move on, you see, than to be encumbered by an old man."

But then two young Russian soldiers stumbled upon Apa, and they came to his aid, cleaning his wounds with water, keeping him warm with blankets, and carrying him to the hospital, where he remained for over a month. The soldiers visited Apa often, taken with his humor and charm, not to mention his fluent Russian. They spoke of life rather than war, of home rather than race.

"These homesick young boys looked to me like a father figure. They risked their own lives to help me."

When Apa was released from the hospital, the soldiers whisked him off to a train station on the southern border with a sad farewell.

"You see, my children, without two brave and compassionate Russian soldiers, I would be dead."

A week later, Hwan hobbled out of the hospital. Like Apa, he leaned on a cane and walked with a permanent limp, but he was alive. Nonetheless, it wasn't long before he fell into a deep depression, yearning for the old days and drinking rice wine to numb his pain.

The price of freedom.

As much as I loved Hwan, there was nothing I could do to lift his spirits. Besides, we had other struggles. Food was running out. Meanwhile, my brother drank. While Hoon did everything possible to keep us afloat, even selling my dowry on the black market, Hwan sat at home, a miserable soul.

11

THE KOREAN WAR

I watched Hoon disappear on the street.
Had I known he would break his promise, I would have
never let him go.

We settled into what we hoped was a temporary situation, living in a church basement in the heart of Seoul and counting the days before we would return to Sinuiju. By day, Apa gave sermons, and by night, he prayed. I helped the church coordinator with outreach activities. Whenever the church hosted an Open Meals night, a rush of orphaned children would come through the doors. My heart sank for them and for Oma, who would undoubtedly love all of Seoul's orphans and call them her own.

Our basement room was small and windowless, but my Chuseok moon had survived the journey south and now hung on the cement wall, offering a cozy view of home and keeping my fond memories alive. There was also an old piano in the basement, one that Hoon often played at night, lulling me into a deep sleep with Korean folk songs. His music was magic.

I ate most of my meals in the church mess hall, but I found myself missing the Udon House, my favorite windowed table and my long conversations with Hoon.

I missed home.

One evening, Hoon surprised me with a night out. "Where are we going?" I wondered.

Hoon smiled. "You'll see, little one."

We walked a few blocks away from the church and around

the corner to a heartwarming sight—a noodle house! It wasn't the Udon House in Sinuiju, with gleaming ondal floors and warm glowing lights, a sight that had always welcomed me on wintry days. This noodle house had cold dirt-packed floors and a smoky air, and the clientele consisted mostly of men who stayed long into the wee hours of the night, washing down plates of noodles with endless cups of rice wine. Still, it was a nice break from the mess hall.

Like old times, Hoon and I took a table by a window. Outside, Korean and allied American soldiers patrolled the streets, their presence a reminder of imminent war. But look to the stars and we could be anywhere, in Sinuiju or on Sogha Mountain.

With The Hundred Choices Department Store a distant memory, Hwan and Hoon found work. His academic background enabled Hwan to obtain a research position at Chosun Christian University. The longer he worked, the less he drank, and the happier he became. Hoon found odd jobs sweeping floors, cleaning windows and outhouses—anything to help put food on the table. For a man who once ran the most opulent department store in Sinuiju, wearing silk suits and fake smiles, he took on his new role with dignity. While my heart broke for Hoon, there wasn't a time I was prouder to call him my brother.

Letters from both Oma and Ajumah began to arrive in the first few weeks. They were brief, one could hardly call them letters at all, but rather notes. Amazingly, they spoke of all the good in the world. How they managed to remain optimistic was a mystery to me.

Dear Miyooki,

I hope you are well. Your oma and I are fine, keeping busy with the ever-growing number of orphans. The weather is beautiful here, perfect for walks through town. I built a vegetable garden in the front yard. Soon we will have cucumbers and tomatoes.

Please take care and look to the stars.
Love,
Ajumah

Oma's letters were no different.

Dearest Miyooki,
How is my lovely daughter? Is the weather as nice in Seoul as in Sinuiju? Life is calm and peaceful here. Ajumah and I have been quite busy gardening and making food for the orphans. So many mouths to feed! It's always nice to see their smiling faces as they devour their meals.
Say hello to everyone.
Love,
Oma

"Spies open all mail," Apa told us. "The purpose of our letter writing is to let our loved ones know we are still alive."

"One wrong word could mean a death sentence," Hoon added.

And so, for each letter I received, I wrote a response, which was brief and similar in tone.

It was just as well, since there was precious little good news to report anyway. But like roots to trees, Oma and Ajumah's letters grounded me amid turbulent times and made me believe we were still a family unit.

Then, one day, the letters stopped.

I worried but continued writing letters to both Oma and Ajumah. Weeks passed, then months, and even years without receiving another letter. Still, I kept writing, perhaps in vain, but it was my way of keeping Oma and Ajumah alive. And yet, in my heart, I had given up hope of ever receiving another letter from them again.

At the age of eighteen, having passed the entry exam with Hwan's help, I enrolled at Ewha Womans University. But before I could settle into college life, war broke out on the peninsula.

The year was 1950.

"North Korean soldiers are swiftly making their way south," Apa said. "They are murdering young South Korean men along the way."

"Why only men?" I wondered.

"Because young men represent the biggest threat to their victory," Hwan said. "Hoon must go to Pusan as soon as possible."

Most young men had the same plan. The seaport town of Pusan, on the southern tip of the peninsula, was a safe-haven where an American base was located. Due to his permanent limp, Hwan was deemed a harmless cripple and safe from danger. Hoon, however, a strapping young Korean male, was perceived as a threat to the new regime in the north.

One evening, Hoon and I went to the noodle house. I ate slowly, savoring the moment. I didn't know how many more meals we would share before he left for Pusan. Just the thought of him leaving brought tears to my eyes.

"Why are you crying, little one?" Hoon asked, trying to remain cheerful.

"I don't want you to leave," I said.

"I'll be fine," he insisted, but his chopsticks trembled in his hand as he ate.

When our meal was over, we walked back to the church. Hoon paused at the gate, and my heart swelled with panic. "Go inside now," he said.

"Hoon, where are you going?"

"A boat is leaving for Pusan in a few days," he said. "I'm meeting with someone tonight who might be able to sneak me on the boat before it leaves dock."

It was an eerie, starless night, and I could hear distant gunfire, and see smoke billowing above the mountains against the black sky.

"Don't be late," I said, worried.

"I'll be home soon, little one," he promised.

I watched Hoon walk down the street, fading to a mere shadow. Had I known he would break his promise, I would have never let him go.

EPILOGUE

A knock at my door brings me back to the present. My daughter is here to lament about her restless son. Unlike Hoon, who never came home that starless night, shot dead by North Korean soldiers, I will remind my daughter that Carson will be back soon, when he is ready.

To this day, I remain heartbroken over the war that destroyed my family. While I miss my beloved husband—who I followed to America, and who blessed me with four lovely children of my own and died much too early—that is another story for another time.

Soon after arriving in America, Apa died in his sleep. I was told it was heart failure, but I was certain it was a broken heart that had killed him. Hwan lived a long and quiet life, working as a researcher at the university and marrying a nice Korean woman who worked at Ewha. Together, they had six children and twelve grandchildren.

I never saw Oma and Ajumah again, a divided Korea sealing our fate. But I still think about them every day. I think about Song-ho, too. Not the soldier, but the boy with the blue-stained arms and sad eyes who had loved lemon candies.

Yet it is the memory of my beloved brother, Hoon, that always brings a lump to my throat. If I close my eyes, I can still see him working The Hundred Choices Department Store floor with flair and elegance. Yes, a bygone era, but one always alive in my heart.

ACKNOWLEDGEMENTS

Thank you, Justin, for loving the book title before a single word was ever written—your enthusiasm was infectious. Thank you, Skip, for manning our chocolate shop when I dove deep into this book—your unwavering commitment gave me the time to write worry-free. Thank you, Francie, for always nudging me to submit my work—your unceasing belief made it happen. Thank you, Jaynie Royal, for being my fabulous editor and publisher—your hard work and dedication are unrivaled. Thank you to the entire Regal Team for transforming my manuscript into a beautiful book. Lastly, thank you, Mom, for making this book possible—your vivid memories and intricate storytelling were mesmerizing.